SYNOPSIS

Once again Grey's team of seven Trippers travel from 2114 to 2014, although only a layover, it is an important one, they would not have been able to complete their previous mission without it!

After a quick task, the Tripper team continues backwards in time; to a period that has them dealing with the spies, espionage and smuggling of the world war one era.

Europe is in turmoil, creating opportunities for those with an entrepreneurial mindset and a flexible moral system. All bets are off as the team does whatever it takes to accomplish a multifaceted mission the world will never know about, but will reap the benefits of, from now till the end of time.

KANGAL

C.M. Halstead

KANGAL
Book Two of The Tripper Series

Copyright © 2016 C.M. Halstead

Cover design by Ted Ruybal, Wisdom House Books.

Manufactured in the United States of America
For information, please contact:
CM Halstead at cmhalstead.com

ISBN-13: 978-0-9863445-5-8 Paperback

ISBN-13: 978-0-9863445-4-1 Hardback

ISBN-13: 978-0-9863445-6-5 Electronic

LCCN:

FICTION / Science Fiction / Thriller / Adventure

1 2 3 4 5 6 7 8 9 10

To Linus,
for teaching me unconditional love.

SPECIAL THANKS

To Tonya, Alex, Scot, Steve, Shelly, Matthew, Junel, Dina, Kevin, The Sages, and for the editing prowess of Megan West & Kathy Bazan.

Special thank you to Ted Ruybal of Wisdom House Books for his awesome cover designs.

CHAPTER ONE

She sits there in her own waste; having no choice, she is starting to get used to the idea. Hands bound behind her, with chains that are threaded through a metal ring in the wall, she has no ability to stand or move. About all she can do is lie down left or right; either way, her now ragged dress and its extra contents would come with her just the same. Might as well sit up--it seems to smell less, and be more tolerable in this position anyway. Not to mention, any blood that is flowing from her face has a better chance of finding its way down her throat, instead of across her face and into her eye. Knowing nothing about the amount of blood her body contains, she is looking at it as a victory over the government that turned against her and locked her in one of its nastiest prisons. It seems it is their strongest desire to deplete her of all her blood and will, through repeated beatings.

Having been here for over a month, she now knows exactly what she is accused of. . .not a good time for it either. France is looking for scapegoats and culprits as to why they are doing so badly in this war against the Germans. She of her frequent travels and ability to spend time with people of power, and is willing to do so regardless of their nationality. She is driven solely on a monetary basis, not on a belief system or nationality basis. This is what made her most dangerous.

Naturally she was a spy, or at least the perfect scapegoat that no one would miss, to take the fall as one. After all, those powerful men will just replace her with someone else; she has no internal lies about her status in societies. Just the best paid concubine they will ever have had is all she is. Unfortunately, that won't be realized until several years from now, and she will be long dead by then. Im visse', she will be dead by the end of the month, if she is lucky to live that long.

*****

At the top of the stairs and down a long dark hallway, not far from where the woman slumps tied to the wall, a key scrapes its way into a rarely used lock. The lock screams its protest and is used anyway. The key turns and stops, a little more pressure is applied and the cylinder reluctantly releases with a click that rings down the hallway. The sound, travels the hallway to the woman. In spite of being beaten severely and starved of food or any sustenance other than water (that was more piss than anything), she kind of hears the noise in the back reaches of her brain. Ears swollen shut from a cane's blows, she feels the sound more than hears it.

The heavy door groans profusely as it is pushed open, the sound echoes indefinitely.

Whispering...

A scuff of a boot on a step, then another and another, reaching the bottom of the stairs, a pause.

Someone talks quietly, under their breath, "He said right." A scuff of boots that turn into

Click

Click

Click, click, click... the sound is moving confidently toward her.

It's about this time she manages to lift her head. It takes a minute or so to get it high enough to be able to look. When she manages, she sees shiny black boots standing there totally out of place in this dungeon. Working her head higher, she sees that the rest of the man matches his boots. Totally put together and perfection through effort, she has seen many a man like this before. Most of her powerful customers had at least one of these guys hanging around. The men were the kind kept around to handle things that are not happening, and never did--the kind of things that would ruin reputations, and powerful men. Therefore, these men are kept around to do things that most are not capable of.

He speaks, "You awake?" He cocks his head and looks sideways at her a little bit, waiting.

She manages to nod her head a bit.

"Good," he says.

"I am here to present you with a choice: stay here and die, or come with me, and help redeem yourself in the eyes of France."

He stands and watches her as her head sways back and forth, half from semi-consciousness, and half as a reaction to her body's pain. They obviously have been working her hard.

He crouches down onto his haunches, moving himself to her level. He does his best to make contact with her.

"This is a one time offer," he says.

He tries to look into her eyes but they are so swollen he can't tell if she can see him or not.

"If you help me catch a spy, we will release you from the accusation of being a spy and set you free."

The man waits patiently.

He hears a whisper.

"Yes."

"Yes, I will do it," she whispers....

Quieter, almost not out-loud, "I will do anything," she says.

He watches her fall over on the straw.

Over and over she says this phrase, not aware that she has actually passed out and is dreaming the phrase in her brain.

He watches her for a moment, trying to see what men see in her. It's hard to tell in this state. Mostly, he likes her tenacity; it may come in handy too.

The man calls for the guard. He works his way down the stairs and hall quickly.

"Yes, Mr. Batard?" he asks.

"Carry her out of here and get started cleaning her up. I will send my doctor," Mr. Batard says.

"But she stinks and is filthily and is. . .probably disease-ridden."

"And that is all your doing." Mr. Batard says. After a thought, "Carry her out of here. Now."

The guard reluctantly moves towards her and after unchaining her from the wall, he picks her up and throws her limp body over his shoulder. As he bounces her a bit to reposition her, some of the waste escapes her dress and falls to the ancient straw.

"Misfortunate suisje," escapes the guard's mouth as he walks down the hall.

The man, Lee Batard, stands there watching the guard and his half-dead package moving down the hall. He then listens to the guard's boots scrape as he ascends the stairs towards the fresh air and light above.

"You have no idea, my man, no idea at all, how misfortunate you really are." Lee Batard smiles, knowing the guard will be killed as soon as he reaches the automobile. We can't have any witnesses, now can we? This didn't happen after all. Looking around in distain, he marvels that this woman; this Mata Hari is as tough as she was talked up to be. Surviving in this environment for as long as she has proves it.

Amazingly, she confessed to nothing the entire time she was here--not even things they know for a fact she did! This is exactly why he needs her for this gig; no other can pull it off. She is dead anyway. He can just return her to here when he is finished with her. Then, she will be able to finish her job as scapegoat for France.

Getting a whiff of the freshly fallen diarrhea, he steps over it. With purposeful strides, he charges down the hall, hoping it will be a long time before he has to return to reclaim anyone. Yet knowing this war is just getting warmed up, he is sure he will be here often over the next few years.

CHAPTER TWO

John arrives at the rookie meeting first. Grey is already in the ready room, waiting.

Grey looks up, "Hey John, welcome back. How were the days off?"

"Good! I slept a lot, ate a lot. Wondered and thought about things," John replies.

"That last part is dangerous. We will talk about that a lot won't we?" Grey asks.

John just laughs.

After a moment of thought, Grey decides this is a good time to do it, "Since you here are early, let's do this now." Grey stands up. Reaching into his chest pocket, he searches around for something and finds it, "Put your hand out, John."

Obliging, John puts out his right hand.

Grey hands him something, or more accurately, places something small in his hand. Looking down, John sees it is a patch of sorts. Picking it up with his other hand, he takes a closer look. It's just a rectangular piece of patchwork, same color as the back patch on the tripper suit. Almost indiscernible on the piece of cloth is the classic skull &

crossbones. The only addition is two little lightning bolts coming off the skull at apposing angles.

John smiles, "Seems appropriately small...like to not make a big deal out of it, just part of the job." He looks up at Grey, feeling a little emotional, something he's not really capable of, yet it is there just the same. "How many do you have?"

"A few." Grey responds, "Like you said...it's part of the job. Regardless, it is a big deal of sorts: can you imagine the regular people out in the world putting their lives at risk for an unknown cause?"

Easy answer for John, "Not really."

"Exactly, the whole signing the blank check thing is a rarity John, even if the person is doing it just for the fun!" Grey smiles, knowing John's journey to the team--how it all started by joining a revolution out of boredom and a need to feel alive.

Smiling himself, John asks, "You mean like the old slogan, 'Thank a Vet. They once signed a blank check to their country.' Is that what you are talking about?"

"Yes, you did the Carte Blanche thing and you know it!" Laughing Grey continues, "You are the clique of 'great white savior!' You had it all and you left it all for a cause, and now you are in on an even bigger cause--even if it's for fun. Personally, I think doing what you love is a great idea. It staves off the thoughts of retirement, which to most people just translates to: waiting to die."

"No way, Mr. Grey!" John's replies, "I'm with you on that. I'm not waiting for anything."

It's at this point in the conversation that June and Mackenzie walk in the door smiling and talking. Seeing John and Grey standing there, facing each other and looking at them, they stop in their tracks.

"Are we interrupting something?" Mackenzie asks.

"Feels like a moment or something," June adds.

"Not at all, ladies! Come on in! Grey was just handing me a way to keep track of all the times I wake up to Charles' ugly mug! John says. Can one of you sew it on for me?" he asks.

Suddenly they both look solemn, not the effect John was going for.

"Which reminds me, actually!" John walks around to the back of Grey. Grey's attention follows him, of course.

John makes his way to behind Grey. He scopes out the huge patch with the overwhelming image of a warped crazy clock with legs, arms and eccentric hair, Running into a worm hole. The motto, "Been then. It's different now" adorns the bottom in Latin. Across the top of the patch is the motto, "We go in together. We go out together." It is along the top edge of this slogan that John focuses his attention first. Scanning with his eyes, it takes him a second to pick out the patches, such is the subtly of them.

"1, 2,... 6, 7, ...9, 10. Ten! Holy shit, Grey, you've woken up to Charles' ugly mug 10 times! Amazing!" He finds himself trying to imagine that feeling 10 times over. John supposes he could get used to it, but still hopes he doesn't have to. Maybe he can help the Tech guys figure out a better way.

Mackenzie and June join him in the close inspection of Grey's back patch. Other than being slightly more worn than the rookies, it's pretty much the same as theirs. Remember, these suits are about bombproof, so wear and tear isn't much of an issue. Who knows how long Grey has been wearing this one. Knowing him, he wears it all the time!

"What are these?" Mackenzie asks. She is the first to notice the myriad of patches located around the edge of the back patch. There seemed to be about six other patches: three of them distinctly different and another three alike.

Grey answers, "Depends on the ones you are looking at. There are three that represent the team members I have lost and the others are for specific events or times. Those three are long answers for another day."

Taking a step away from the three rookies staring at his back, Grey pivots on one foot and turns. He is facing them instantly, but is now about three feet away from them. He needed to create some space.

Motioning to the table with his hand, Grey says, "Let's get started. Everybody sit." Going to pull out his chair, he changes his mind; they have thrown him off his game a little bit with their childlike curiosity. Each of those patches represents a traumatic event of sorts, located on his back. He doesn't think about them much. It's a good place for them--behind him.

"Let's grab four chairs and sit out here where we are standing, instead of at the table," Grey grabs two chairs and places them where they are standing. Mackenzie grabs the other two and places one for her. While placing the other chair, she looks at John and motions for him to sit there. Saying thanks, John sits without any of his usual inappropriate comments. Grabbing the chair to

Mackenzie's left, Grey manages to make eye contact with her. Just one moment of eye contact to say, "See I told you: no wise ass comments signals that he likes you."

As Grey sits down, he has the thought, "If she put the chair down for him, does she like John? Who knows? Who cares? Let's get down to business!"

All four sit facing each other. June sits to John's right and Grey's left. There are no barriers between them.

"OK, rookies," Grey says, "now is the time to ask the questions that have come up since we last talked or any unanswered questions from our last mission."

John jumps in first, of course, "How's it work? The time travel I mean."

Grey answers, "I'm not really sure to be honest. You may find that out before I do John, with your ability to intermingle with the technicians, maintenance types, and scientists."

John wonders how he knows about what he has been doing with his time and asks him so.

"Everything we do here is recorded and analyzed. Don't worry too much about it though. We would have to do something pretty out of character and extreme for anything to come of it. Just know that anything new and different will be brought to me by report, just in case. Key here, is, to me, that the system itself, decides whether to send it, and it will come to me first. I will either come to you if it's something to address, or delete its existence. More than likely, it will be the latter. No one else gets to see or know. That is what I believe at least." Grey says, "Just remember, I am on your side and get the big picture of things.

"Like knowing that you (pointing to John) have an in

with the geeks of world is an advantage to our team, here and on mission. I will do nothing to deter it."

As soon as Grey is finished, John asks the next one, which is burning a hole in his mind, "Why we do it? Travel back in time, that is. What's the purpose of it?"

Grey answers, "Damn John, we covered this, didn't we? At least once!"

John, looking sheepish "I know, I know, but I just want to know! It's part of who I am."

Grey gives him his final answer, "Last answer of this one John.

"If we spend our time trying to reason why, instead of doing, we will drop the ball, screw the pooch, tank, or any other cliché you guys can think of. If we are thinking about repercussions and results for others, we will be distracted and not be present on mission; this leads to your friends and team members, as well as innocents, getting hurt.

"There is an old saying, 'ours is not to reason why, ours is...'"

Always impetuous, John interrupts Grey, "to do or die. Got it! Doesn't mean I have to like it, Mr. Grey."

"Likewise John, I don't always like it either. Someday we will be old and retired. We can sit around and banter through it all; in the meantime, that is someone else's job. And if it all gets crazy and doesn't feel right, we will address it at that time," Grey says.

John looks at Grey, perplexed, mostly because he can't believe what he just heard from Grey. That phrase is the beginning of a bigger issue. Maybe Grey does know more that he says, and is capable of thinking against the system.

While John is thinking, June speaks up, "What

happened to the scientists?" she asks.

Grey says, "I am not privy to the details of what happened, or is happening with the scientists. It's always good to assume the best for them, not the worst. I've only had to bring a few live beings back over the years, and a lot of them I've run into at a later date. You never know, if you use the public cafeteria, you may run into them at breakfast some day. Again, don't think about it too much." Grey grins genuinely: having broken in rookies before, he knows he will have to say it frequently for about a year.

"Is there death on every mission?" June asks her other burning question.

"More often than not, to be honest," Grey says looking at her. "It just seems to be part of what we do. Sometimes, it's because we are being forceful, like on the last mission. Other times it is, I don't know how else to say it, a byproduct of what we do. I'm not going to justify it or try to give examples, just know it is not my first choice, not my preference. But if it becomes a choice between mission success and failure, then it's a no-brainer for me. This includes our standard rules of engagement: we are not there and never were. We will do whatever it takes to ensure this part of the mission, up to and including terminating anyone. In some cases, they will force it upon us."

"Who is 'they?'" June asks.

"They would be: bodyguards, armies, sheiks, dictators, street punks, housewives with shotguns. If one of us is captured, interrogated and happens to confess, then we will have to deal with that situation as well."

June gasps!

John laughs, "He doesn't mean whoever confesses, but

rather who heard the confession."

"Exactly, we don't kill our own. Simply hogtie them and bring them back for the PAB's to deal with if they go off the reservation, break our code, or whatever," Grey adds.

"Still..." June adds, "It's not that I'm against the killing per se, just that some might be innocents, just living their lives. We happen to come along and intermingle with them causing the termination of their lives! It's nothing they did."

"True, very true, June," Grey responds, "Just like someone killed by a drunk driver, caught in a crossfire, or eaten by a shark. It all just came together for that situation to happen, and it just is. It was supposed to happen, that is what my brain tells me, at least."

June is obviously dealing with some moral dilemmas. Hopefully, it is just about the possibilities of hurting innocents. Grey's instincts tell him this is true. She is a confident grifter, and is just dealing with moralizing her new life with her age-old morals.

"How about you, Mackenzie? You have been quiet; any questions, concerns, or comments even?" Grey asks.

"Not really, I am more the one to go with the flow for a while and see what it is all about before forming judgments and questions. I have been coached all my life and am familiar with going with a new system, before judging it," she says.

"What I would really like to talk about is, how different this is from what I am used to, and speaking of confessions, I have one of my own," Mackenzie shifts nervously in her chair. She had hoped that when she had this conversation, they wouldn't all be staring at her while sitting in a circle. But perhaps this is best. "I want to say how awesome it is to be sitting here with you and I wish the others were here, but perhaps it's easier with just you three. Grey, you may already know, but John and June don't. Before I lose my nerve. . .I need to confess that the rumors are true. I killed my husband. I know I just blurted it out, but there it is."

John sits back in his chair. No other movement in the room.

"I killed him because he cheated on me with just about everyone. I never thought I would do something like that. I never thought he would do something like that, but he did. He slept with all the other starting members of my team. Apparently, I wasn't enough. He also slept with my agent and various other women over the years." Mackenzie filled them in on all the gory details of his multiple indiscretions, some of them with her in the next room at the party. "Apparently, he had all the discipline of soccer fan, whose team just won the season and finds himself in the midst of violating his home city. 'I don't know how it happened' may be an appropriate answer to trashing a city, but not to sleeping with twenty plus women. It was his 'I don't know why I keep doing it. I just like it,' reply to my question, 'Why he did it?' that set me over the edge. I beat him to death with one of my trophies. I was awaiting trial-- literally I was in the holding area of the courts--when the recruitment team showed up and gave me an offer I couldn't refuse," she says.

Nobody says anything.

Mackenzie continues, "I just needed you to know, because I wanted you to hear it from me and not to find out, when I wasn't there to tell you why and present my case, so to speak. I'm not saying it was OK--my actions that is--just that I felt THAT betrayed. It was a complete betrayal of trust for me. I was so mad...." She pauses to look up; she had been staring at the floor the entire time.

Mackenzie, feeling her shame, has been unable to look them in the eye and forces herself to do so now. "I also need to say, that I already feel different with this team than any other team I've ever been with. I know it may be hard for you to feel comfortable around me now, but I still needed to come clean. I don't want to be like him and hide stuff. I trust you all already, after less than a year, and hope you will trust me in spite of this," Mackenzie says.

Done with her confession, she sits silent. The entire room is silent for what seems like forever.

John speaks first, "I trust yah."

He makes eye contact with her and smiles. "I trust the confession, for sure. Talk about putting it out there. You just place all your cards on the table, face up!" he says.

June doesn't say anything. She too is staring at the floor. Probably thinking about how ironic it is she is worried most about killing innocents, and then Mackenzie's confession. It is a true perspective on how life is not black and white. Not that she will condone death by anger, just totally feeling the brutal heart blow that Mackenzie received from the one she let into her heart most. June will have to remember not to let any of her marks put her in their hearts. The grifts must end before that happens.

June reaches over, grabs Mackenzie's hand and gives it a squeeze. They can talk later; this gesture is perfect for now.

"Ok, good stuff rooks," Grey says. "Now, how about next mission. Who wants to hear about that?" He looks over at Mackenzie and smiles reassuringly. He of course, already knew about her story and demise in her previous life.

Having need-to-know privilege, Grey has access to anything he wants in regards to his team: the past records, current records, and the computer's information it has gathered on them from the past, just before they deleted it all. The only records that exist on any of the Trippers are contained within this facility. They do not exist on record anywhere else in time. The only thing that can give their existence away would be paper records, photos taken by friends and family, things like that. Even those only hold a little weight, this day and age. Any of those things can be created, manipulated, changed, or anything else you can think of. If we don't exist in computer history, we don't exist at all.

Grey brings them up to speed on what is to be their second mission, "The next mission is a little more complicated than your first. We will be going back to the barn we went to on the last mission, and then after a recharge and a short mission, probably accomplished by John and Charles, we will do another jump further back in time. All told we will be about 200 years back in history from today.

"June, you will be pretty integral to the second part of the mission; you and Charles in fact will be attached at the hip, so to speak. You will be using your persuasion skills and he will be your body guard. No more details than that until we get to our first jump spot," Grey says.

"Mackenzie, you will be laying low with me and Rosa at the first jump, while John and Charles go accomplish something. When we get to the 1900's, you and John will be working with Miokel on a back part of the mission. Don't worry, it's a very important part of the mission. Both teams will need to succeed in order for it to go as planned," Grey says.

John asks, "What happens if it doesn't go as planned?"

"Then we regroup and formulate another plan," Grey answers. "We will always accomplish our mission, one way or another. Now, with that being said, on a very rare occasion, we return home." He puts his arms out to make sure he means back to home base. "We return home, regroup and do it again. Sometimes with the same exact plan! The privilege of being able to travel through time is sometimes, on rare occasions, we get a do-over."

The three rookies smile at this.

"OK," he continues, "that about sums it up and since there are no more questions, get out of here. Your itinerary for tomorrow will be on your in-room computer as always. You are free to go workout, play, sleep, read, whatever."

"But I have more questions!" John says.

"Of course, you do. We will chat later. Get out of here, all of you, we are done." Grey gets up and puts his chair back to emphasize his point. "Go play and have some fun. That is an order!" he says.

Grey walks out of the room, leaving them to figure it out. Nothing good comes from lingering in his mind. Besides, he has a long list of things to accomplish today. They are the ones that get to play.

C.M. Halstead

CHAPTER THREE

Round two with this girl was unexpected. This guy he has been watching is not known for extended relationships, and neither is the hooker riding him. After a break and a conversation, they decided to have at it again, this time with her on top. Having seen her perfect breasts from afar, there was no blame to be found.

Taking his eye off the scope, he looks at his watch. Charles is on a schedule today. If it wasn't for that, he would just sit here smoking and watching the show. Unfortunately, the overachiever in him scheduled another hit for this afternoon.

Frowning at his watch, Charles settles back into his primary position, sitting in a chair with both feet planted. He relaxes his posture back into its comfort spot, his eye naturally resuming its position behind the scope. He can see the sweat glistening on the prostitute's back as she works the man. She is striving to finish him off and the man is helping her along; hands on her waist to move her at the perfect rhythm while she gyrates him into her.

Suddenly, they stop.

She sits there, long enough for the man to say

something to her while he puts his hand over his eyes, she nods and dismounts the twice gotten-off man. Walking to the window, she pulls the curtain closed.

Damn!

Charles once again glances at his watch, cursing himself for making assumptions about how quickly this hit would be and his choice to schedule another this afternoon. This one he could have done tomorrow; the other is leaving on a jet, never to be return.

He sighs and resigns to the decision that just ran through his brain. Standing up he quickly disassembles the custom-made Dragunov. Pulling the PSO-1 optical sight off, he pulls the pin on the quick disconnect stock, and then the magic barrel release. Putting it all into the made for this purpose cello case, next he pulls the magazine and clears the round in the chamber. He double checks the chamber, ensuring it is clear. Charles places the round back in the magazine, while placing it in its foam formed spot. He snaps the case closed. Since he did not use it for the hit, he will keep the rifle setup for a rainy day.

After a quick scan around the room, he makes for the elevator door. Since the apartment is no longer in the picture, Charles makes sure traces of his presence are non-existent, before entering the private elevator to the parking garage.

Charles wants to move fast. He hates the idea of not being able to see what his target is doing. He knows it will take him approximately five minutes to get to the target's door. The target probably won't leave in that time-frame but the hooker might, and she was intended to witness the shooting. One would think that wanting an innocent to witness a murder was cruel and mean, and maybe it was, regardless the contractors wanted it as part of the deal.

Usually people want to hide assassinations but in this case it was a setup. A rival takeover is in action and the current second-in-command is the stoolie for the unknown client.

Charles has to get over there now! Since he wasn't able to off him while the girl was in the bed with him, he will have to go with the back-up plan: planting evidence for her or someone else to find. The informants will take it from there.

The elevator reaches the parking garage. As soon as the doors open, he is off to his vehicle to place the case in the trunk. In a hurry, he hoofs it up the short flight of stairs in order to cross the street. Jay-running, he dodges the minimal traffic passing through this high-end neighborhood, and gains the few steps to the entrance of the Brownstone.

Entry is but a few seconds delay, the codes already provided in the job packet. Glancing at the elevators on his way by, he sees neither of them in motion. Smiling, he pushes open the door to the stairwell, and takes the stairs two or three at a time, arriving at the 3rd floor about a minute after the 1st. floor door closed.

Glancing through the door's classic small wired, diamond shaped window, he sees no one in the hallway. The target's apartment door is shut tight as well. Resigning himself to the fact that he may have to be seen, and come face-to-face with the intended screamer, the body finder; he opens the door from the stairwell, while locating the copied key in his chest pocket.

Approaching the apartment door, his senses are up, listening and feeling for any movement along the entire floor as he approaches. Stopping just to the side of the apartment door, he listens as he puts the key in the lock. Hearing nothing, he turns the key and door knob together while entering the apartment.

Pausing to listen before closing the door, he hears a shower running and a man humming; these sounds appear to be coming from two different places. Good, this helps out his plan.

Closing the door, he places the key on the floor and proceeds towards the humming sounds, scoping the apartment as he goes. Listening and feeling, he gets no alarm bells as he walks, and pausing just outside what should be the bedroom he was watching from afar; he listens one more time. He could hear the man on the bed breathing, and the woman shutting off the shower. He knows the bathroom entrance is right next to the bed. He is out of time--he must do it now!

Charles breeches the door, not hard since it is open. Hurrying, he rushes the bed. The man looks up from his euphoria, losing it to the sight of Charles heading his way--knife in hand, urgency in his face.

To the man's credit, the freshly laid sod reacts quickly and leaps off the bed in time to meet Charles' charge, face-to-face. His semi-hard-on bounces in protest as the now adrenalized and endorphined man leaps at Charles, attempting to take him down. Charles manages to redirect his charge by using the man's energy against him: he simply sidesteps the charge and implementing a neck manipulation, flips the target flat onto his back. The target lands solidly, knocking the wind out of his lungs. Before the man can even start to gasp for air, Charles is on him. If one were watching, it would appear as a frog-like action. His effortless leap and just as perfect landing, places Charles' butt on the man's chest. With a leg on each side of him, knees firmly applied to the biceps, the man is pinned to the ground.

The man, a whirlwind of confusion, has no time to think about how quickly his day went from perfect to craziness. Being well trained, he was able to get to his feet and apply a charge at this intruder; if he wasn't still panting from his morning hooker romp, he would've heard this guy's entry into the apartment. Doesn't really matter what he would've done, at this moment he is being held down by someone who easily gained that advantage.

As he calms himself to allow his lungs to recover and start breathing, the man above him reaches down and wraps both his hands around his neck.

Instantly, the thought, "Oh, thanks be to God!" rampages through his head because, for a fleeting moment, he thought he was about to be pummeled to death. After all, since he had done the deed himself more than once, he was acutely aware of what a brutal way to go that is. Grateful at his misfortunate fortune, he turns his remaining thoughts, not to whom and why someone has sent a hit-man to kill him--he knows someone else will spend time on that--but rather how awesome today's boobs looked while they jiggled and bounced. He had given her financial incentive to get him off quick; the quicker he came, the bigger tip she got and she went all out for the extra cash.

Charles slowly increases the pressure around the man's neck, leaning into him a bit, not so much that he loses his center and gives the man an advantage, but enough to secure the death choke. He knows that with blood unable to reach the brain, this man will be dead in a matter of. . .just a few more...seconds. Charles looks into the dude's face, waiting and watching for the life to leave his eyes. Just before it does, the man smiles and then his eyes go blank; apparently, his last thought was a good one.

Charles starts to contemplate what it was when his thoughts are interrupted by an ear piercing scream! The prostitute has opened the bathroom door! Looking up, he sees her standing there, horrified hands to her face, already dressed for her departure.

*****

Charles sits up rapidly, his heart beating as fast as humanly possible, the sweat river and his confusion at a high point. He looks up at the woman looking down at him.

"It's OK, Baby. It's OK," she coos as if to soothe a fussy child.

Her hands are out in front of her, gently waving back and forth in the air as a sign of calming and passive protection. She is smart enough to be out of reach and this forces Charles to take a second to focus. As he does, his eyes clear. He sees who she is.

He was dreaming again. Dreaming about one of the hits gone wrong. There were only a couple that didn't go as planned and, all things considered, this one didn't go all **that** wrong. There was a hooker left as a witness and the target was killed. It's just that the hooker saw his face and because of that, he would have to leave town or kill her since she was the only witness. In the past, he would have gotten up quickly and fled the apartment. Hookers generally don't want to get involved: if you leave them alone, they will just stand huddled in a corner, hoping for an escape, either before or after your departure. They are loathe to call the police because that calls up so many questions they don't want to answer. Even if this lady of ill repute was questioned by the fuzz, his chances were high that she wouldn't "be able to describe him" in any detail at all. We all have our own survival code, and she wanted to live.

"You OK, Baby? Dreaming again, obviously." That voice from above again. Looking up, Charles sees a woman of exotic decent, looking down at him. With long, dark brown hair, almond skin and round eyes, she was a beautiful sight to be seen. Probably the best post-nightmare sight in the world.

The woman looking down on Charles is someone he has known for quite a while, a long-time friend. Well, long-time friend and former doctor. When he first came to this time, his brain took the opportunity to kick in some serious PTSD. Luckily, the PAB's still believe in the power of the mind, and its influence on the performance of its human carrier. In their ultimate wisdom, they provide each human in this program with someone to talk to. In Charles' case, the first one had been the woman who is now standing above him. They have come a long way from those first sessions many years ago. So far in fact, that she is officially no longer his headshrinker. He had been passed on to someone else long ago--although he rarely even went.

Why would he? This one shows up at his apartment, carrying his meds and wearing awesomely see-through, translucent undergarments for him to watch her walk around in post sex. Her body, perfectly curvy, is accentuated by the gossamer fabric's form and design; for any straight man, it's the best therapy in the world.

Charles rubs his eyes, clearing the sleep and the dream images from them. He takes a moment to regroup and then stands up to greet his friend.

"Hey, you! Didn't know it was that time already. It's good to see you, Angela." He stands up to give her a formal greeting. After all, he is always glad to see Angela. When Charles is with her, everything is A-OK! Grabbing Angela, he pulls her close to him, taking a minute to settle her into the perfect position. Nestled together and completely centered, he looks down into her eyes. They look back at him with that constant blend of concern and adoration. It is her most common look when close to him.

Angela puts her arms around his waist and nests the side of her face into his chest. Getting a perfect location for it, she pauses in order to hear his heart beat. Listening, she hears he is fine. The dream behind him now, his heart beats a perfectly healthy rhythm. Every time she does this, she is amazed at his health; as a benefactor of his health and stamina, she is eternally grateful for it too. Especially at his age, she knows for a fact that he is a 43 year-old man with a life-long history of job-related abuse to his body. His list of unseen internal body damage rivals the amount of scars on his body. Once, she tried counting and stopped at 20 when she started to get that overwhelming emotion that his past brings to her being. At times, her empathy is almost deadly to her. The thing she most wants is for his mind to heal and for him to be able to sleep at night, without having to ingest THC and CBC into his body. It might be a long time coming, never with the kind of job he still has, but whenever it happens, she will be there to feel it.

Taking her head off his chest, she pulls away slightly in order to look up into his eyes. He returns the gesture. They say nothing, just standing there looking into each other for a moment.

A moment is all they can take before disrobing each other and taking part in their favorite intimate thing to do together: slow, steamy, sensual sex. For them, it is all about touching as much of each other's body as they can at all times, while allowing the hands to roam at will. In this carnal dance, they take turns powering the grinding forces unconsciously moving their hips together, each completely in tune with the other.

*****

Charles sits out on his balcony sucking on his vaporizer, while Angela primps herself in his bathroom. She is working on re-hiding that perfect body beneath those consciously boring outfits she wears most of the time. It is a move on her part, to keep her clients focused on the reason they came there, and to help prevent the whole falling in love with their therapist thing. Didn't work with these two, of course--although to be honest--they fell for each other slowly, and more from that one time they ran into each other in the commons. That chance encounter turned into a four hour conversation, culminating in dinner and a night of passion. Charles, one to fall in love with a brain, as well as a body, was pleasantly surprised at what she revealed for him that first night: the perfect body so easily hidden beneath an outfit tailored to produce no type of sexual reaction out of anybody, ever.

Taking another draw off the handheld vaporizer, he settles in to the chair as the medication wafts through his body. As the THCs and CBCs remove the stress and worry from his body and mind, he calms into a euphoric state. Gratefully sanctioned in this day and age, Charles is a constant consumer of his prescribed meds. This was not always the case throughout history, it just seems like perfect kismet that he now resides in a time that he does not have to rely on Prozac, roofies, or gratuitous amounts of alcohol to sleep--all of which he has tried at different times in his life but each failing in the fact that although they allowed him to sleep at night, they prevented any kind of productive lifestyle while he was lost in their effects. However, 2114's cannabis strains have been tailored to the needs of people like him. Long gone are the times of hippies and sustainable clothing; this once illegal weed is now the natural medication of choice. Charles was told that once the world moved on from, and outlawed any synthetic drug and food of any kind. It was just a short while before medical marijuana came to the forefront of helping humans deal with their natural afflictions including stress, anxiety, and any other of the mind fucks that are an integral part of the flawed human system.

As he hears Angela approaching, he takes one last dose and puts the portable vaporizer down. Standing up, he knows she will have to leave—it's time to go back to her office. He also knows he will see her again tonight, one last time before he goes off on another trip through time.

"OK, Baby, gotta go," she says. Before embracing him, she puts her arms out and asks him, "How do I look?" She has changed back into her professional attire.

"I know your body so well, it's like I have X-ray glasses on when I look at you," he says. "Otherwise, you look perfectly boring in your gray business suit." He pulls her towards him as he puts forth the words he knows she needs to hear. Hugging her close, he whispers in her ear, "I will think of you the entire time I am gone."

"Yes, you will," she purrs as she removes herself from her favorite place, his arms.

"Enjoy your afternoon off. I look forward to seeing you next time, where I will once again be able to transform myself from the quintessential business woman to the sexy beast I keep for your eyes only," Angela teases.

Smiling, he pulls her towards him again, "I love that part of you and your culture," Charles says.

"What's that?" Angela asks.

"That I am the only one who gets to see your perfection. All others only get your perfect mind. I get it ALL," Charles smiles at her, his eyes lighting up mischievously.

"I like it too. I am happy to save it for you, my dear." She smiles at him and pecks a kiss onto his lips as she pulls away and heads for the door.

He watches her leave, wondering if either of them will ever allow something more than friends with benefits.

Doubtful.

CHAPTER FOUR

The colonel stands to shake Grey's hand as he enters, "Good morning, Mr. Grey. How were your days off? Relaxing, I hope. What is it you do on your days off? Don't worry, I ask all my guys that. Just helps me get to know you better...and yes, I have a habit of asking several questions at once!" Colonel Petzer says.

Smiling, the colonel sits in his desk chair and motions for Grey to sit in his soon-to-be, usual spot.

"I don't do much, sir. Mostly, I just relax and watch mindless entertainment while reading any good fiction I can get my hands on. That, or utilizing the virtual vacation system," Grey responds.

"I remember, you don't go up top and take a (the colonel puts his hands in air to make air quotes) live vacation, do you? Preferring instead to stay down below and utilize virtual."

"Have you ever used virtual, sir?" Grey asks.

"No, I haven't," he replies.

"It's amazing, sir. The body is all driven off the brain. It's the control center--the nerves, muscles and electricity of the body all flow through there. If the brain believes and experiences something, then it happened in the body. I wake up refreshed or exhausted and sore, depending on what I chose to do."

Grey grins mischievously, "Anything is possible in there."

Looking at him, the colonel smirks, "I will have to try this virtual vacation thing soon!

"But first, down to business. Your team does indeed have a mission, and it is a double trip. Something else for me to learn, how that works, hmm. I will have to visit Loren again on that," the colonel says.

Colonel Petzer removes a small notebook from his chest pocket. The best way to keep things a secret in his world is to write it down and put it in his pocket. After he is done with it, he burns it so the only version that exists is whatever his aging brain remembers, and gaining access to that will never happen. He would shoot himself in the head before allowing that or scramble it so they couldn't gain access. He sticks the small pen back in the spiral and puts it back in his pocket.

"As I was saying, it's a double trip." The colonel picks up a folder off his desk and reads it to Grey, "The first part is going back to the same location your team tripped to last time. You need to acquire that vehicle which you used on the last mission. It says…" The colonel looks up from the folder at Grey, "Guess I need to get used to stuff like that. Care to explain?"

Grey clears his throat, "It's hard to explain, sir. Logically, you already understand or you wouldn't be sitting in that chair. It's more about how our brains have a hard time accepting the reality of it." He looks at Colonel Petzer, trying to figure out what he is thinking, "Pretty soon all this stuff, all the missions that you send us Trippers on, will become the norm, and if you happen to have the opportunity to interact with people out in the world, their lives will seem surreal and strange! The normalcy and linear way of their life will seem so boring and illogical. It's part of why I don't go up top. There's no sense to it."

The colonel knows Grey is right. Having 20+ years dealing with special missions and forces, he knows his reality is entirely different from that of those to whom he reports and for whom he works. The military liaison and political interaction level is unique as well. Speaking of a politicians deal with perception and perceived possibilities, while the colonel's troops have always dealt with tangible cause and effect. His new troops still do--just with a longer, less quantitative effect.

The colonel thinks for a moment to that meeting he had with Loren, the lead tech on Grey's last mission. He is the one who showed him the data stream and thinking area of the system. Loren was able to put in layman's terms what the computer bots and information worms are up to, and how they gather their data from current and past data streams. It is a hard concept to grasp, but like Grey as stated, the brain only has to accept the reality of it, change its learned way of thinking, and expand to accept the concept of time travel. The long-term effect of a small tweak in a moment of time has a huge effect 100 plus years later.

The colonel finally responds to Grey, "Point taken James, point taken!"

Grey jumps slightly--there is that reaction to his first name again (less than the last time) yet still there.

"So your first mission on your layover," the colonel smiles at his own analogy, "is to locate, purchase, and then stage the vehicle right where you found it previously."

The colonel throws a folder across the table to Grey. "Inside are the particulars of where you can find it, along with the money to purchase it."

Opening the folder cautiously, Grey glances through it casually--more to ensure everything listed on the need list is there than to read the details of it. Inside the file, he sees two mission write-ups and several packets of currency. He notices more than one currency. "That's right! This is a double trip, isn't it? Love it!" Grey pipes up. "That means I get to go way back in time!"

Colonel Petzer smiles at Grey's enthusiasm, "You like that part, don't you?"

"Yes sir, it's quite the eye opener, that time travel," Grey smiles mischievously. "Especially to see humans in times before high technology and worldwide social systems were possible. The thinking is a lot smaller and less linear in its cause and effect."

"What do you mean?" Colonel Petzer asks.

"If you are from now?" Grey asks, fishing for an answer. The colonel says nothing so Grey continues, "If you are from now, you have always had the mindset that world is small and connected. We all know the cause and effect of the consumption of resources and sustainable numbers of humans etc., without the emotional attachment that the people had 100 or 200 years ago about managing the human population levels. The concepts and practice of population management have been taught in schools for at least 50 years now, before that it was considered sacrilegious--or worse."

The colonel interrupts, "Yes, I grew up in a time of Bio-monitoring for health and ZPG, the standardization of population control. It is amazing, actually, at one time population growth was the mission of many a country and religious belief system. It was a way to strengthen their culture. The smart ones even had lack of birth control and survivalist practices built into their agreed way of being. Can you imagine that now, in a time of zero population growth!" Colonel Petzer laughs at the thought, "Um, yes ... Mr. James Grey, I have asked you here today because you are slacking in your reproduction quota. If you don't step it up, we are going to find you a few more wives!"

Laughing, Grey also shudders at the thought. Not one to let people tell him what to do, he can only imagine what would happen to him in a situation such as that. Not to mention the thought have having WIVES (plural). He is perfectly content in his bachelor life.

Grey says, "I don't think either of us would thrive in a situation such as that, sir. We seem to be of the independent thinker sort."

"Yes indeed, James, yes indeed," the colonel says.

Colonel Petzer continues on with the mission brief, "OK, second mission is a lot further back--1917 it seems. I've read the packet and am not sure of the big picture part of it. I'm thinking, when I get to see the results of the mission shortly after your return, it will make sense to me."

Grey raises his eyes at this. Mr. Roberts never mentioned that, never mentioned that he got to see the results. Grey always assumed only the PAB's further up the food chain were privileged to this information.

"There isn't much I can say to you about the results: that is need-to-know information," Colonel Petzer says looking directly at Grey, "But I did want to let you know that I am privy to it. I have let the other trip leaders know as well. Apparently Mr. Roberts wasn't one for full disclosure. I am."

"I appreciate that, sir, and I'm fine with need-to-know boundaries. I keep my team in the dark as much as possible for safety reasons, if nothing else." Grey says.

Colonel Petzer, reading through his copy of the brief, falls silent for a moment. Looking up from the file he says, "It appears we will really be breaking in your grifter on this one. Seeing as how it is only her second mission I want to ask, is she up to it?"

Grey takes a moment to read the file.

After a few minutes, he looks up, "Yes, sir, she is up for this--especially with the body guard in play with her. She is not much of a fighter, so that part is helpful.

"Yet, she does seem to have a tremendous influence over people. Instantly in fact." Grey gives him a few examples from the last mission, specifically the winning over the guards instantly part.

"Perfect, she will do well," Colonel Petzer responds.

"So, yes. Yes is my answer. She is a young 30, and yet still wise for her age. She will excel in this job for sure. June will just need to toughen up a bit," Grey says.

"And will!" the colonel responds emphatically.

*****

Grey decides to take a risk and ask Colonel Petzer the

hard question, "Sir, you seem to be the sort who respects those of whom you are in charge, and correct me if I am wrong, you also seem OK with an open banter between you and at least your team leaders. I'm not saying you are open to a member of my team coming and chatting with you candidly. Especially John, I definitely don't recommend an open banter with him," Grey says, blushing a bit at the thought of John speaking his piece to Colonel Petzer. Knowing John, he would ask him if he had any daughters or something intrusive like that. Realizing he softened his bearing, Grey continues, knowing his body will move on from the blush quicker if he continues, "I wonder what you think about Mr. Roberts. I know you didn't meet with him more than a day or so, but I wonder your opinion of the man?" Grey asks.

All of the sudden there is a faint buzz in the room. It is located in a back corner, something is buzzing around in the shadows, doing its own thing. Grey hears it first and Colonel Petzer moments after, based on his reaction.

Keepings its beady eyes on the two humans, it scopes around, looking and listening. Waiting for the perfect opportunity to sneak in when they are not looking, it waits until they are distracted by whatever they are doing. Now! Eyes watching, listening. It works its way in behind the human with its back to him, using him as a block to the other's vision, it sneaks closer to its desired target.

Colonel Petzer answers Grey's risky question, "I would agree with what you just said, James. The fact that I want to call you by your first name in these meetings proves that fact. So, I am glad that it is working. The message is coming through.

"As far as Mr. Roberts, he wanted me to call him 'Andrew,' but I didn't. I didn't feel comfortable with him enough to do so. There is just something about him I don't trust," Colonel Petzer says. "He is of a different sort, more politically minded, maybe even of the spy mindset. Somehow, he weaseled his way into this program." The colonel continues, "You will have to get more and more accustomed to dealing with the likes of Mr. Roberts. He will surely keep gaining power somehow. I can tell he is one that will--one way or another.

"You will also have to deal with the PAB's. I will force you to do that soon. Your experience with this program is valuable and I want to use that to help deter any resistance to increased funding. Even in this day and age, there is intense competition for financial resources," the Colonel finishes.

That annoying buzz is back.

Having no choice but to swing right a little, the fly veers slightly. A direct route is too obvious: it likes to sneak up on its intended target and circuitous routes are best for this.

Grey hears the noise directly behind him now, perfect in his blind spot.

"Even this," Colonel Petzer puts his finger in the air, waving around him, "isn't impermeable. Even in this impenetrable structure, the natural way prevails: outside things find their way in on occasion," Colonel Petzer warns. "Mr. Roberts, believe it or not, actually disclosed that to me. . .I have the few files on the incidences. My favorite is a (using finger quotes) 'Lost hiker' I didn't know they still existed; who is crazy enough to hike about in the wasteland above us."

"Don't know, sir, but the point is taken. Even in this impenetrable structure, the natural way prevails," Grey says.

A moment of silence.

The varying buzz in the background is the only noise in the room and it keeps gaining their attention. All other sounds are constant: the hum of the air flow system, a computer off to the side spinning its fan, Grey and the Colonel's breathing.

Both the breathers sit and wait for the fly to find its way over to its intended target, a half-eaten pastry sitting on the desk that waits to be finished. Filling the air with sweetness, it has nothing but enticement and lures the fly out of its hiding place.

The common fly works its way around the human closest to him; in a circular motion, it makes a run for the pastry. The fly flies wide around, just out of the humans' range of vision, flying lower and lower as it goes, intending to get below its target and come up and over the desk at it. At the last moment, it loops its flight up the edge of the desk. The scent of sugar overwhelms the fly as it puts down its landing gear. Sugar is a drug to the fly, as addictive as crack cocaine. His brain cells implore to him that he must get a fix--in spite of the danger.

Just before the fly can land, a huge hand swipes at it, forcing it to make a hard left and then circle back right, so it can come back around to the sugar's location.

Must have it, the fly's brain says! It comes back around to land on sugar, this addictive siren.

Another hand comes at the fly; in mid-air, the fly puts on the brakes and flies backwards in avoidance. Abject and utter failure: the fly is engulfed by the human hand!

Clenched in the human's fist, the fly is shaken back and forth violently. Then, with one last motion, the fly is flung down onto the desk, tantalizingly close to the sugar-filled pastry. Confused, the fly tries to decide what to do, all the way down to…

When the hand hits the desk with force and violence, the lights go out for the fly. Bam!

The colonel looks disappointed, "I missed but you didn't. Nice catch."

"Thank you, sir. Out of practice?" Grey asks, giving him an out.

Colonel Petzer laughs, "Yes a little. Not for long, though."

Looking at the dead fly, Grey says, "In regards to what we were talking about before our hunting expedition began, I know we have to, I have to. Like you said, I've reached the level where I cannot be oblivious to the PAB's goals and intentions. Pretty soon, this new team of mine will be ready for more 'present time' missions and I will have to make decisions based on their current dogma."

"Be prepared to run into contradictions on occasion as well. Not to mention amateur crews. It is getting more and more affordable, and easier than it used to be to fund," Colonel Petzer says.

"What is, sir?" Grey asks.

"The technology to produce short trip machines is now

affordable to the top 1%, not just the PAB's," Colonel Petzer declares.

Grey is a little confused, "I'm under the impression that the PAB's are the 1%'ers," he responds.

"Even they have a hierarchy and in-fighting. They are competitive humans, after all. Just because one guy gets the final say, doesn't mean they all agree to it. And if you have the ability to go back in time, even a short while, that can give you an advantage," Colonel Petzer says.

"So you mean even if the PAB's send a crew back 100 years, these guys now have the ability to go back, say 10-20 years and try to change something back?" Grey asks, "Well I don't mean change back but..."

"Influence," the colonel finishes Grey's sentence. "Or kill off even, I know our recorded history doesn't show it, but there is a battle going on behind the scenes; sometimes, it is a literal one."

"That's good stuff, sir. Thanks for that tidbit. I can tell you will be more beneficial of a leader than your predecessor, and I mean no disrespect to the recently departed Mr. Roberts," Grey blurts out.

The colonel can't help but smile. "Good, that is my intention. I am glad it's working already." Pausing and looking at Grey, "And don't worry, I'm sure we will run into Mr. Roberts again at some point and time. My instincts tell me so."

He looks at Grey, wondering what he thinks of that statement.

Grey nods his head subconsciously as he realizes he knows it as well. He is pretty sure it won't be under good circumstances either. That guy always seemed more of a politician or spy than a military-minded and mission-minded man; Grey agrees with that. Colonel Petzer is definitely the latter kind of man though, making him better suited for their missions.

The colonel lifts the cold cup of java to his lips and looks at the dead fly on the desk. Mr. Roberts will not be as easy to stop as the fly--if he does reappear.

Placing the coffee remnants back on the desk, he picks up the fly and puts it in the trash receptacle in the wall behind him. The slight vacuum pulls it from his fingers and whisks it downward out of sight.

"I have nothing else for you, James. Anything else for me?" Colonel Petzer asks.

"Just one unanswered question, but it's really for someone else I think. HR for policy? Yes? One of my new Trippers is looking to go into town and I want to make sure he is good to go."

"Is he good to do so?" Colonel Petzer asks.

"Even though he is one of my rookies, he is actually," Grey answers. "I know he hasn't been here long, yet he is ready. He is from about 60 years ago, and yet seems to grasp today's world very well, at least the down here version. I think when he came from is pretty similar to how it is now. Way more tech driven but the hierarchy was just the same, chosen and unchosen, two- tiered society. Except he was one of the chosen and left to be one of the rebels, sir. Says a lot about him, I think," Grey comments.

"It also means he will probably do well in both the under and over-worlds of now, and of recent years. Used to the obviousness of it, that is," the colonel says.

Grey nods even though he doesn't know exactly know why the colonel says this.

"So that's it for me, sir, unless you have anything else?"

Grey asks.

Colonel Petzer lost in thought, thanks him absentmindedly, and pointing at the door, gives his answer.

Getting up, Grey thanks Colonel Petzer, and exits his office. Tipping his hat to the gatekeeper, he finds his way to HR. It has literally been ages since he's had to go there. Reluctant to do so now, he tells himself he will make it quick and dirty. Rush in. Ask his question. If the answer isn't forthcoming, he will leave his contact info and they can get back to him.

*****

Rounding the corner of the hall, he sees the world famous "Human Resources" sign hanging above the second door to his left--the sterile, gray-edged, black-faced and white lettered sign of every government establishment since the invention of placards.

Opening the door, Grey enters and ignores the sudden stares and looks of the half dozen people waiting. He walks up to the counter, still feeling their looks of awe, envy, and fear upon him. It never leaves him: the notion that although these people are here to support the Trippers' mission, most of them still don't know what to think of Grey and the other Trippers. Somewhere on the spectrum between fanatical and crazy is a lot of their perception whereas Grey and most Trippers think it is the people who are crazy. How can you just sit at a desk all day, or go to the same place day after day after day, doing the same things? All are needed he supposes. He is just glad of who he is and hopes they are feeling the same way about their choices.

Grey looks through the looking glass into the next room, where the HR personnel are cordoned off from the outside world, purely to keep their information safe.

The room is descent in size. The walls are thick and soundproof, not a sound can be heard, creating a surreal feeling to anyone looking through the glass. One can see a multitude of actions taking place: conversations babbling along, mad typing, several personnel walking back and forth and yet none of the normal office buzz makes its way to his ears. The only thing he hears is the silence of the people behind him, either still staring at him or flipping the pages on their digital pads. It's so quiet a finger swipe can be heard.

Suddenly, a comely, middle-aged woman appears on the other side of the glass and looks up at him. She, a mere 4'11", has to crane her neck to make eye contact with him. Like many others, she takes a step back in a futile attempt to see his face because his beard is obscuring her view.

Her voice comes out of two cones embedded in the wall on either side of the small window well, startling him in stereo. "Yes, sir, how may I help you?"

No other sounds escape her side of the glass.

"Yes, I have a question from one of my new Trippers I need help answering. He wants to know at what point he is able to..." She raises her arm suddenly and puts her hand between her face and Grey's, raises her index finger and says, "Wait one."

She's obviously dealt with his kind before.

"All tripper questions are addressed by Junel. She handles the Trippers," the woman says.

"That's a little bit of a misnomer, don't you think?" Grey says.

The woman smiles mischievously, "We'll see." Grey sees her mouth say as she motions to him to go to the door to his left. She meets him there and opens the door for him. She surely knowing he is standing there ready, even though he can't see her through the solid door. Using his senses to search for the cameras without looking, he thinks he has located them above him, in the corners of the small alcove created by the door entry.

He walks through the door.

Waiting for the door to close, she then leads him around the corner and down a short hall to an area encompassed on all sides by glass offices. The center section is about three times as wide as the hallway they just walked down, and full of motion and noise. Grey surmises that the offices on the outside probably hold managers and other keepers of even more secret information than the rest of the people in this lockdown section.

Scoping the room, Grey notices there are five offices per side. There are just as many in the middle area, albeit cordoned off from each other with waist-high cubicles instead of floor-to-ceiling glass. Perhaps each office denizen is rated an assistant of sorts.

The woman with no name leads him to the third office on the right, stops just past it and turns to him, putting out her arm as if to motion politely, "After you."

"There you go, sir. You will find her in here."

Grey says, "Thank you, mi lady." He enters the office ceremoniously.

Entering, he feels the woman behind him walk away as

he scopes the contents of the office. The back two thirds of the office is of solid wall construction; the other third is of that aforementioned heavy duty glass, creating an open feeling.

Although he can see down from one end to the other of the office block, he can hear nothing outside of this room. Somehow, they have created a sound proofing of sorts without a closed door.

Looking about, he sees normal office furnishings although no notes of personal touch are within his line of sight in the office. Once he really looks at the woman behind the desk, all else is lost to him anyway.

Had to be a blonde, didn't it? Grey muses to himself as he stands there unmoving, saying nothing.

The woman behind the desk is working like mad on something--typing like she is a jackrabbit escaping ravenous predators. Focused on her work, she doesn't notice him standing there at first.

Grey smells her suddenly: the clean, womanly essence of someone who spends an hour or so each day in front of her primping station, applying several layers of lotions, cleansers, and finish layers. She exudes an awesome blend of scents. Some of his favorites, actually: there is a whisper of citrus and a spice which lingers luxuriously around his nose. Looking closer at her, he is memorized by her long, straight blonde hair. Those strands not controlled by her hair clip, escape in thick strands. Unimpeded, her blond hair cascades freely, making its way down, past her shoulders to her back and the areas in front of her shoulders. A few wisps move about slowly in the slight breeze caused by the air system. His eyes move to the area where they should not be and he gets lost in the cleavage managing to escape from her jacket and blouse. Pushed out in front of her, there seems to be ample amounts to take turns escaping.

Her posture is perfect as she works. Her back off the office chair in a perfect S-curve: she must have trained herself to do this instead of the standard computer slouch of most. This pushes her chest out, giving Grey a perfect side view of the curvature of her fullness. Ample and full, he is doomed. All thoughts of his purpose elude him for a moment as he stands there taking her in.

After a couple of seconds, his presence is realized by Junel. With her attention deep in her work, she did not hear this man come in. She is startled to find this tall, big presence of a Tripper standing there checking out her breasts. She leans forward in her chair and looks up at him.

"You alright there, tough guy?" she asks.

He laughs. She got him. Good for her!

"Yes," Grey responds.

He recovers quickly. Sitting down in the chair next to her desk, he enters her space without permission. She sits back in her chair.

John's request will have to wait. Grey needs to have some fun first. "Rumor has it you get to be the HR contact for the Trippers. How is it you came upon this auspicious job? Did you fail too many exams? Or perhaps, piss off your father or, wait I know, you made Mr. Roberts angry. That's it, isn't it? You told him 'no' or something, didn't you?" His mock interrogation gets to her.

Blushing slightly, she says, "Definitely the last one--on more than one occasion. Usually it's arguing with him about burnout and the repercussions of pushing Trippers too hard. Too many suicides, you know petty stuff like that."

"I knew it!" Grey exclaims. "He is gay! If that's the only thing you had to say 'no' about."

She laughs.

The unsaid joke hangs heavy in the air.

Leaning back in his chair, Grey takes a really good look at the woman sitting behind her power desk, seeming vulnerably human and impenetrable at the same time. He bets she would make a good Tripper. Except he doesn't sleep with Trippers--too complicated! This one, however, has good potential.

He introduces himself, putting out his hand, "I am Grey," he says.

She takes his offered hand.

"Good to meet you," she says. "My name is Junel."

"Before I get distracted by conversing, I do need to ask you an R & R related question about one of my new guys," he says.

"Ok, go ahead, Mr. Grey," she says.

"I have a new Tripper who is requesting to go up top. He is from 2054, so he is used to a two-tiered society. He has been here about eight months and is raring to go party with a couple of my experienced crew members. The kicker is, those two like to hang out in the lower tiers, and this new guy is from the upper tiers of his time," he says.

"Do you trust the other two? And how about we use names? This is human resources, after all. What's said here, stays here," she says.

"Sure, Rosa and Charles are the seniors and..."

"John is the new Tripper." She interrupts, knowing his

crew. "Do you think he is ready to go up top and see what it is like this day and age?" she asks.

"I do," Grey answers. "And I think he is super curious and bullheaded, and may try to talk those two into taking him either way since he has the thought in his head. So I want to make sure he is copasetic to do so. This is the first time it's come up so soon."

"So wait, you've been a Tripper for how long, Mr. Grey?" she hits a few keys and looks into her computer for the answer. Her eyebrows go up when she sees the answer.

"A long time, Ma'am," he answers.

"Right and you've never asked this question before or it's never come up?" Uh oh, her HR voice is on.

Laughing, Grey answers her, "Right, it's never happened so early that one of these guys wants to go up top and leave this world. Usually they are content learning how everything goes down here and in the traveling they do for work. This guy is, well, this guy is..."

She looks into the screen, and there go those eyebrows again. "Narcissistic, computer genius, grew up rich and led the good life. Bored, he chased ladies and joined a revolution."

"All reasons he'll make a great Tripper, Ma'am." Grey adds,

"He's a quick study, wants to succeed and will be just fine up there, especially with Rosa. She will set him straight."

"So is that a 'yes,' Mr. Grey?" she asks.

"Yes Ma'am, that's a 'yes,'" he says.

"Why do you keep calling me 'Ma'am?'" she asks.

"Why do you keep calling me 'Mister?'" he replies

"Out of respect," she answers.

"Out of respect?!!? What? Are you calling me old?" Grey is becoming indignant.

She inhales deeply, "No, sir, I am not."

"Oh, so now you are calling me 'sir.' Well, you are calling me old? Is there such a thing as age discrimination these days? Can I cry wolf or just plain ole give you a hard time?" Grey asks.

Though confused and not knowing where to go from here, she is usually adept in dealing with these Trippers and fast talkers. This one, though, he has been here since before it all began and yet, he is lithe and young of face and mind; his beard, as long and as gray as his name, is all that gives him away.

After taking a breath to gather her wits, she says, "I would say, if you think he is ready, then go for it. Let him do it and then check in with him when they return, Mr. Grey."

"Well, Ma'am..." he drawls.

"Why do you keep calling me 'Ma'am?'" Flustered she is.

"Why do you keep calling me 'Mr. Grey?'" he retorts.

"Respect for. . .for time in," she answers wryly.

Ugh, she just called him old again.

"Likewise, I am sure," he answers.

Getting up, Grey puts out his hand for her to shake it. "Thanks for your help, Ma'am. I appreciate it."

She shakes his hand. He thinks she is holding it a little too firmly and a little too long for a purely professional office hand shake. Hummmm.....could she be...?

"You can call me 'Grey,' by the way," he says.

"You can call me ..." Shit! I am supposed to be professional. What do I do?

While she is thinking on that, Grey says, "You can get back to me on that." He lets go of her hand and walks out.

Wow, that happened! Grey walks down the hall—struts, actually. That woman has awakened his libido. It's been awhile since he last remembered feeling it. Most women he lets into his world are stunning--the kind other people can't help but check out even in his presence (much to his chagrin). He has to resist the urge to pummel them instead of just enjoying the fact that they are envious of him. Someday that may go away. Then again, maybe not. He kind of enjoys it in a way.

Who cares! In this moment, shut up... Wow. Is all he can say. He is glad he did well and planted some good seeds with her.

"I will look her up after this mission, for sure," he says to no one in particular.

On the way out through the door from the inner sanctum into the lobby, he manages to glance up as he exits and notices small holes probably containing the cameras above him. Tucked up and out of sight of a person approaching the door from the waiting room, they can be seen on the way out--if you are looking for the possibility of them.

Walking back into said waiting room, Grey spots three of the same people waiting and a couple of new ones. Those three are either security or have a long wait ahead of them. It would seem to him that they are security, as one of the new people in the waiting room gets up when her name is called by an unseen announcer. The original three show no signs of that dread disease, waiting room impatience so they are definitely working.

Grey grabs the door handle and opens it. The chaos of the hallway blasts its noise into the quiet ambiance of the waiting room.

Stepping out, the door clicks shut behind him. The plastic sign looms above him, swaying slightly from either the air movement caused by the door shutting or the ventilation system.

He decides to head to his apartment for some downtime before locating John and having a one-on-one with him, unannounced and unofficial. If he wants to go to the next level so quickly, then the two of them will.

CHAPTER FIVE

June and Loren sit across from each other, separated by a spindly-legged bistro table.

When June arrives, she consciously sits across from him--she needs the table as a buffer. Used to people not being able to let go of her, she wants to set the tone. She has had a couple of scary incidents: one with a boy and one with a female friend of hers, both were very toxic and would not allow June to remove them from her life. It is times like those that she is grateful to have run in the circles that she did. Even then, it took a couple visits from the right people to convince that woman to relocate. She just couldn't live in the same area without following June around all day, every day. Charisma can be a curse, after all.

Very quickly those fears are alleviated with this one. Loren is not like that. He seems happy and ecstatic--not so much about the breakup, but that he was with her in the first place.

In his excitement, he is in ramble mode, "...and then I went back to my apartment, thinking maybe you would be there, naked on the couch waiting for me. Instead, I saw the red envelope on the cold unit, and I knew it was from you. When I walked to it, there was a part of me that knew it was a breakup letter, but the optimistic side of me was thinking it was a love letter and you had left me instructions on where to find you, and it wasn't until after I opened it that all those unsolved mysteries in my brain about your strange smells and weird hours suddenly were solved, and instead of being mad, I was grateful to have spent all that time with you before you fully transitioned to the Tripper lifestyle. After all, I may be the last relationship you ever have," Loren says triumphantly.

June's tremendous gasp interrupts his constant flow of words, "What? Why would you say that to me?" she asks.

Loren is shocked out of his excitement at getting to speak his piece to her. "Well, because of what you said. Well, not just what you said, but because you are right."

"Right about what!?" she retorts.

Realizing he has hurt her feelings, Loren chooses his words carefully, "As you stated in your letter left on my fridge, 'The Tripper life is not conducive to a relationship', not a direct quote but something like that," he says.

"I didn't say ever!" June responds. "I said while I learn it, and get used to the constant travel, and new way of life. I didn't say I wouldn't ever have one, or that we couldn't ever work out," June says, exasperated he didn't get the unwritten part of the message.

Loren sits back in his chair. He had been excited and sitting on the edge of his seat while speaking his piece; now that she is reacting to what he said in a defensive manner, he slides away from her unconsciously. "June," he says slowly.

"Don't 'June' me! Why would you think I would never

want a relationship? Do you think I used you? Do you think I don't care about you? Hell, I was falling in love and that is why I set you free!" she says.

"You were falling in love?!?! So you set me free so I wouldn't get hurt? How does that make sense? Why are you care-taking me?" Loren asks her.

"Because. Because, well I don't know!" June is suddenly confused. She had been so sure of her actions and intentions when she wrote the note. She was sure it was the right decision, Now that she is sitting here in front of Loren, she is reminded of what she is falling for. He is one of the rare people on the planet who is able to call her out on her stuff. Somehow, he didn't just turn into putty in her hands--like most men do.

"Exactly," Loren continues, "You ended our budding relationship to protect you as well. You are falling for me and are afraid of what the future brings. Or maybe in your case, what the past will bring into your life." Loren reaches out and puts his hand on hers, "Not like your past, but the past, like from the missions and..."

"Got it!" She interrupts him, anger seeping in her voice.

They spend a few moments in silence. Then she speaks, "I hear what you are saying. I'm sure you are right. I was scared and am scared to be attached to you with all the unknowns in my life. I have no idea what the future brings--and not to mention most of my relationships have actually been grifts."

Loren looks at her shocked, the worst images going through his head.

Quickly, June assures him, "I didn't sleep with them. Don't worry. It didn't have to be like that in my time frame. At least, it wasn't for me. Maybe it would've progressed to that but being so young, it wasn't a huge issue. They were just happy to have my attention. Plus our grifts were super-fast: we figured the less time in, the less chance of getting caught. Get in and out before those doubts start appearing," June says.

"Well, that doesn't work for me," Loren says. He looks her in the eye. Taking his hand off of hers, he sits back in his chair again. He says slowly, thoughtfully, "...And I want to keep you in my life. We obviously have a connection, and even right after our breakup (he uses hand quotes audaciously) we are able to communicate. That is pretty rare, I would say!"

Loren smiles at her.

June looks up at him.

Her head down looking at her hands, just her eyes come up and the look of despair slowly leaves her face. A smirk and then a smile. Feeling a little happier, she sits up straighter in her chair, "What are you trying to say?"

Loren responds, "I AM saying we should remain friends. I know you will disappear frequently and often. Keep in mind your time gone feels to me about half of what the time line is for you. I don't want to bore you with science and math, yet it's good for you to know there is not a direct correlation between your experience of time while on mission, and our current time here. There are a lot of weird idiosyncrasies that crop up all the time."

June reaches out to touch his hand this time, "And that is why I like having you in the tech center. I feel safe knowing you are there keeping track of everything and making sure nothing goes grody on this end."

"What does that mean?" he asks.

"Messed up and out of control. Basically making sure,

nothing goes technically wrong. You know that stuff is alien technology to me," she says.

Laughing, Loren says, "Thanks, June, I appreciate that."

She relaxes back into her chair, "So now what? Where do we go from here?"

Loren laughs again, "How about we just go with the flow and make it up as we go along. Cool?"

"'Cool?' What does that mean?" She might not have heard the term on any of her jaunts through time and is not getting his expression.

"It means: Are you OK with it? Is it all good? Do you agree? Need I go on?" Loren smirks at her.

"Yes, I am OK with that," June smiles back. This guy is different. He is capable of being friends with her and not freaking out. He will be good for her; indeed, maybe even help heal some of those old stalker wounds. Maybe he is the rare person who is able to control himself around her. How awesome would that be!

Suddenly remembering something, she looks up and makes eye contact with a woman sitting at another table across the common area. The woman is facing her and sitting with a man who has his back to June.

It is Rosa. June felt the need to talk to someone and told Rosa about what has happened in the past. When June asked her to be there just in case he got all crazy and violent, Rosa didn't hesitate.

"We are in this together. Remember?" Rosa spoke like a protective mother bear and then she added, "I'll bring Charles with me for good measure. He and I are headed up top for a bit like we always do. We will meet there before we go. Just let me know when! Charles doesn't even need to know what is going on," Rosa said to June.

Grateful to have her there, June smiles at her from across the commons. Rosa smiles and gives her the thumbs up with a question on her face. June continues to smile and nods to Rosa. Rosa puts her other hand into a thumbs up and smiles back at her lip syncing just one word, "Awesome."

June continues to watch for a moment while Rosa says something to Charles. They both gather up their stuff and get up to go. Charles looks over his shoulder and winks at June-- apparently Rosa told him or he figured it out. Knowing Charles, he kept track of everybody that came and left this area during the time he was here. Not much gets by that former hit-man. Surprised, she is not.

Focusing her attention back on Loren, June sees him turning his head back in her direction, after discovering what she had been looking at.

"A back-up plan, huh? Do you really think that little of me?" Loren asks incredulously. Smirking at her, she knows he is partly kidding.

"Well in light of our recent agreement, I think I should tell you about some things that have happened to me in the past. Would you like to know?" She asks of him.

Loren responds, "Absolutely, please do tell."

They settle in for a long conversation, perhaps something they should have done previously.

CHAPTER SIX

Walking out from the commons, Charles and Rosa head for what they call the escape hatch. There is only one central area with access to up top. "Up top" is what everyone who lives down here in the concrete encasement calls the surface of Planet Earth. There are some here who, once they committed to the project, have never been back up top. Grey is a great example of this. The reasons vary: lab rats rarely leave their labs anyway. Some are in hiding from commitments or trouble up top. Others, like Grey, see no need to spend time up in that world and way of life. He, like some others, is completely content to live encased in concrete when not out on mission--something that people like Grey actually consider better than living up top.

Charles and Rosa are not two of those people: they like to go up top at each and every opportunity. Over time, they have learned the best places to go and play. Together the entire time, they are a formidable force for any mischievousness that may come their way.

Partners in crime from the first time they met, one must only look upon them to come to the conclusion that they are buds of the highest caliber. No need for sexual tension or brotherly/sisterly love, these two are partners in crime, cohorts and cronies of the greatest kind. Their mission when up top is fun and frolic. May the gods have mercy on anyone who gets in the way of their mission!

Rosa and Charles arrive at the processing area. After a quick pass of their hands under the security center scanner, they are whisked--with VIP treatment, of course-- through the processing area over to an express elevator. Have no fear: they are still required to walk through the sensors that tell them and the security personnel watching, more than they ever wanted to know about their bodies' nooks, crannies, and crevasses--not to mention any living things currently carried outside and under their skin (a skeevy thing, for sure).

Having passed their clearance and health checks with flying colors, Charles and Rosa settle in for the seemingly long ride to the top. Both fidgeting in their civilian clothes, they constantly adjust their clothing and Rosa fixes her hair, as they kill time on the ride up top. They are unsure whether their discomfort is from lack of time in this type of clothing or from having to stand still, semi-captive, in this elevator speeding to the top.

Both are attired in the utilitarian clothing of the unchosen society--formally known here as Tier One. Tier One clothing is various shades of gray in color and is derived from a blend of fabric that might be as bombproof as the Tripper suits. This clothing is also hard wired for various reasons, mostly having to do with biomonitoring, not resuscitation and communication.

Every time they go up top, they are reminded of how different today is than the late 1900's, the era in which both Charles and Rosa once lived.

Charles and Rosa are from a time when. societal mobility—either upward and downward--was mostly in the hands of the individual and was dependent on two simple things: motivation level and intelligence level. Either of these were enough to gain status as far as money, property, and possessions were concerned. Factors such as alcoholism, drug addiction and just plain laziness were enough to move a person down the societal ladder. Up or down, it was all up to the individual and their belief system, whether they believed it or not.

The society of 2114 is entirely different. Neither Charles nor Rosa know when it all changed, just that they were told today it is all determined by computers. The computer decides if someone goes into Tier One or Two upon birth. Tier One is the unchosen, manager, supervisory, worker bee, or lower type class. Tier Two is considered as the upper echelon of the society.

This rarely changes: mostly, once you are in, you are in until death. Then the algorithms kick back in again to re-balance the population on each tier.

*****

Arriving at the end of their speed ride, the elevator doors open to reveal a transfer area of sorts. Knowing the drill, they head for the helicopters located in the center of the giant multi-use area. They will take this hi-tech transportation up and out of the hidden area that is the entrance to their world below.

Not only is the world below hidden, but the entire transfer area as well. If one were to look up and around, they would see nothing but concrete and air moving systems inside the giant concrete structure, reminiscent of American sports facilities and the ancient coliseums of Rome. Unlike the Roman coliseums and exactly like the American sports domes, this place has a giant roof that opens and closes effortlessly as the transportation and supply choppers fly in and out.

The helicopters seem to fly in and out effortlessly as well. In fact this entire area is surprisingly free and clear of noise and chaos, specifically engine noise. If one were to travel here from the 20th. century, it would seem things just moved around, as if picked up by some giant invisible hand and placed in its new location, or lifted off the ground from above and pulled up and out before the other hand slides the door closed. Occasionally a slight whine can be heard as one of the choppers lifts off or lands but that's about it.

Even the elevator seems to be devoid of mechanical means. Up top is different indeed.

Charles and Rosa are intimately familiar with the noises of the giant machine that creates chaos, vibration, and noise as it goes about its work, sending them to times unknown, while up here everything seems to move about through sheer will.

Neither Charles nor Rosa are the scientific or nerdy type; either would have a hard time describing the idiosyncrasies of a present day engine and why it is so quiet. They just know that all one can hear around here is the scrapping sounds as a helicopter's landing skids leave the concrete or when it settles in on the surface again. The only other sounds here are the idle chatter of the humans contained herein.

Rosa and Charles wait until they are beckoned over to a waiting chopper. The only passengers, they climb in and chose seats on opposite sides of the helicopter. The basic design of the transport helicopter has not changed since the 1970's: big sliding doors on each side and a similar size opening off the back, accessed by a lowering ramp instead of a slider. Each of the three doors can be opened at any time, including in-flight. Back in the day, Rosa spent some time rappelling and speed roping out of the side doors of beasts similar to these. There were those Marines crazier than her who would just leap out the back into waters below. It is people like this who help her feel sane by comparison.

In the front of the chopper is a pilot and co-pilot because no other humans are needed. The door gunners and cargo attendants have become a thing of the past, both replaced by automated systems. In fact, if this complex wasn't such a secret location, the pilots themselves would be a computer. The problem with computers is that they communicate back and forth at will. A record of these trips would soon accumulate and be discovered by the overall system, bringing awareness to anyone who has the clearance. It is much safer to utilize the old school system of having two humans navigate using their sight and experience. Worse comes to worse, they can be eliminated, taking their sights and knowledge with them.

As the helicopter silently lifts itself and frees its mass from the iron will of the Earth, it magically rises and the walls of the structure are soon mostly below them. They quickly reach the top of the structure. The doors above open silently, letting in light and fresh air. As always, the obligatory dust and papers move about the giant building, due to the influx of air currents.

Clearing the roof line, Rosa and Charles finally come awake; they both claim a window to watch something they rarely see while at home base. First and foremost, they see tall pine trees with a deep orange hue to their bark--the trees seem like both giants and dwarfs, due to their location between two immense canyon walls. The tall sandstone walls climb even higher than the 80 meters of trunk that the trees contain. Striving to be clear of the canyon before their death, the Ponderosa Pines have a mere 200 meters to go before they can sneak a peek over the canyon's edges and catch a glimpse of the world above.

As the helicopter rises, the sandstone hues modulate from a orange red similar to the Ponderosa's tree bark, to a milky mellow, more compliant with the shade of benign beach sand. It's almost as if the paint has been washed off of the upper layers and seeped down onto the ground below.

Clearing the canyon walls, the pilot leans the chopper forward as it hurriedly skims the flat edge of the land above. Looking out the sides, Charles and Rosa scope out along the flat edge of a plateau. For the first couple minutes, the surface is flat and seems to extend forever in a northwest and southeast direction, out each side of the chopper. Rosa and Charles know from experience that the plateau is never ending behind them, towards the north as well.

Today as on every departure, the helicopter is heading south towards the mainline. Heading almost due south, one can see a much different and lower type of terrain fast approaching. The helicopter is racing towards the edge of one world, while it strives to reach the other down below. The bottom drops out beneath the chopper. The sandstone cliffs end in an almost straight line to a valley floor below, the sandstone edges abruptly ending at the edge of an ancient lake system, now completely dry and devoid of any water at all.

The pilot suddenly increases the helicopter angle into a dive bomb towards the ground. Both Rosa and Charles grab onto the seats and handles, hearing the laughter and joy coming from the front, they smile themselves. It is a rare opportunity for some G-force fun.

Charles lets out a "Yeeehaaahh" as they race for the ground.

Hearing this, the pilot upfront shouts out to them, "Always happy to oblige my friends!"

Smiling profusely as the chopper heads for the ground, Rosa can do nothing else but hold on as the G-forces increase. Glancing over her shoulder, she watches the blur that is the rapidly approaching ground. At the last moment, the pilot brings the helicopter even with the ground, causing Charles' and Rosa's insides to rise up towards their heads and against their backbones from the all-encompassing G-forces.

Settling into an even flight path, the helicopter allows Rosa's parts to return to their proper places and she is finally able to talk.

"That was awesome, you guys! Thanks as always," she says enthusiastically.

"You bet!" is all she hears from upfront. Rosa knows they are happy for an excuse to use their mad-skills for something other than a normal boring commute run.

"How long this time, guys?" the pilot asks.

"Just overnight," Charles answers.

"Well, have some fun for us, will yah guys? This is our Monday, and we have days before we will get to have some fun and frolic," the pilot says.

The conversation pauses as the two pilots start conversing with unknown voices in their heads, talking them in for a landing.

Looking out their windows, Charles and Rosa watch the helicopter approach the long cylindrical tube below. See through, yet dust covered from the environment, the tough glass is impermeable to any forces that Planet Earth or human beings may throw its way.

This impermeable tube makes a beeline from its location to a huge enclosed city, located to the west. If one were to look east from their current location, they would see the tube going directly into a giant shield-shaped, expired volcano. If the chopper was gaining elevation, instead of coming in for a landing, you would be able to see the tube exiting out of the other side of the ancient volcano as well, heading for lands unknown.

The city is where Charles and Rosa are planning to spend the next 14 hours or so because it is the only officially occupied city in the area. Rumor has it there are many human ruins from several human reiterations scattered about. Every time they come up, Charles and Rosa wonder about their past cities, and whether they still exist or not.

The helicopter lands in its assigned position. Thanking the pilot, Rosa and Charles head toward the passenger platform. They are excited knowing that once embarked, it will take the train approximately one minute to cover the six miles to the city, and within 10 more minutes after that, they will drinking at their favorite spot.

To call this thing they are climbing aboard a train is an ode to Rosa's and Charles' origins. The trains of their time took approximately a mile or so to get up to speed and the same distance to come to a stop. Traveling at a mere 70-100 miles an hour, it would not have enough distance to get up to speed before arriving at their destination.

The train, accelerating to about 600 miles an hour, creates some significant G-forces. Because of this a G-FC was designed, for this and other high speed transits.

The first few thousand human test subjects were never the same after their 0-600 MPH in an instant train ride. It took the computers a couple years to come up with a device that can compensate for the tremendous havoc forces of that type wreak on the human body. Imagine your intestines slamming so hard into your backbone, it causes bruising when the train starts moving and again, at slow down at the other end. The backbone and spine both kept trying to exit the body through the chest cavity and stomach muscles, sometimes succeeding. A horrible sight to be seen, but don't worry, none of the original test subjects lived long enough to develop PTSD or extended back pain, all were dead within a matter of hours.

Thankfully Charles and Rosa will not have to endure this type of pain; instead their bodies will not feel anything due to the G-FC. Essentially a G-FC is a reverse force created by pushing back at the inertia with energy stored from unneeded previous forces; one would need a scientific computer to describe the details. All Charles and Rosa know is, instead of having to fight the god smack hand of being pushed through their seats, they instead feel an equal and opposite hand pressing their backs and legs forward to hold them in place. Opposite is true on slow down, it's almost as if an invisible force is pushing them backwards as the train slows. All of this happens in a matter of seconds.

Regardless, all these two really care about is that they do not have to spend a long period of time traveling to their play zone from their work zone.

*****

The instant the transport doors open, one is put into shock from the paradoxical change. The transport, literally contained in a vacuum, allows no sound to penetrate its protection. Silence shatters upon the doors opening. The quiet din of a motor-less area, nevertheless occupied by thousands of humans, seems overwhelming for a second. After a quick pause for adjustment, Charles and Rosa release themselves from their seats' embrace, disembark, and work their way through the throngs of people.

Looking around, one sees a rather motley lot of people traveling at street level; human power, the only form of transportation allowed at street level, creates a different type of traffic flow: bicycles and skateboards intermingle with each other as they weave their way through the slower bipedal commuters. All seem to be in a dance they have practiced for so long it happens in their sleep, no thought or presence needed as they make motion to their destinations.

Looking up, one can see a transportation system seemingly hovering 100 meters in the air. They are not vehicles capable of flight, the vehicles instead travel on the toughest glass ever invented. Capable of stopping rockets, holding up against the impact of meteors, and strong enough to encase an entire city, it creates an impenetrable sphere of protection to all, and a literal glass ceiling to those below.

The enclosed city of Namazinga-2 is an example of a two tiered society consisting of the chosen and unchosen. Being of a different time, Rosa and Charles are oblivious to the connotations of these labels in detail. Also entitled by their career choice, they have the clearance and carte blanche to go anywhere public, at any level they chose.

Life at ground level--more in line with their lives left behind--is their level of choice.

Already tasting their fun and frolic, Rosa and Charles dash ahead of the worker bees ambling along the same path. In mission mode, they make a beeline through the chaos towards their spot, "The Flashback." Once they discovered this joint, it was a no-brainer that this would be their haunt of choice.

The bar's neon sign flashes slowly, accompanied by the electric sound, synthetically produced to create detail in its ambiance. More retro signs flash in the tiny darkened windows: Budweiser, Labatt Blue and OV Splits all flash their respective, distinctive brand colors intermittently. With their flashing lights, the neon signs seductively beckon every easily beguiled passerby to enter.

Charles reaches the heavy wooden door a second before

Rosa and pulls the door open to hold it for her. Motioning with his other hand, he insists.

Walking in, Rosa is greeted initially with absolute darkness as her eyes adjust to the darkened environment. Dim yellow light bulbs encased in thick chandelier glass embossed with brands of old, hover over wooden booths with high seat backs thus creating private caves for any who sit there. Other than the classic bar games of pool, shuffle board, and darts, the place is barren and open in design. An unfinished wooden floor polished by years of beer, barf, and boots covers the distance between the booths on one side and the bar on the other. Rosa smiles and waves at the bartender as she enters; he waves back jauntily, recognizing his old friends.

Rosa looks around the place. Seeing their favorite spot open, she heads for the booth. You know the one: located in a quiet corner with great visual access to entrances and goings on of the bar itself. Just out of the main flow of things, it creates a private conversation place with access to all the bar's amenities and fun.

Sliding in, Rosa drums the table in excitement as Charles slides in across from her.

"Splits?" he asks her.

"Absolutely, always..." Looking around she spots and makes eye contact with the bartender. He puts his hands out in front of him so she can see them. Using his forefingers, he moves them from a finger length apart to full bottle length and back. Rosa gives him the sign for the little bottles they make there. Every time, it is the same silent joke about how she hates little ones and he points at himself attesting about his being full bottle size. Smiling at each other, they both turn their attention back to what is directly in front of them.

Rosa says, "It's great to feel like a local in a place that reminds me of my early years."

Charles laughs, "I know. Right? Even I feel at home here. It must be that we are of similar lineage."

"Well, some day you will have to let me all the way in and tell me. It's not like they can get to me."

She winks at Charles.

Charles changes the subject, "You off for more of the usual?"

Nodding her head, "Absolutely!"

"OK, I will be right here," he says.

"You're not as fun since you got that headshrinker to deliver your meds and nookie," Rosa jabs.

He gives her a look.

"Just kidding!" Rosa responds.

"No, you're not actually," Charles says. "And yes! I don't need to sleep with mindless hordes of paid women any more. I'm good." He moves his hand laterally to emphasize his point.

After watching his hand move, he looks up at her, sees her smile at him, and smiles back.

"I am happy for you," she says.

Nodding, Charles knows she means it. He wonders if she will ever find someone who can keep up with her. Rosa is a rare breed indeed. Used to being in charge and taking charge of her life. It would take someone of strength and subtly to mesh with her--if she would even allow it. Whenever anyone brings it up, she just states "how busy" she is. If she isn't training or exercising, she is reading--and the gods themselves will need to assist the poor sod who interrupts her while she is reading.

Charles sees her as someone who is set in her ways. She is comfortable with the routine she has and it will take someone superior for her to want to change it.

At this moment, the bartender arrives with a metal tub full of ice and miniature bottles of beer. After sliding it onto the table in front of them, he slides in next to Rosa for some idol chat. Charles takes the opportunity to look about the place; seeing nothing of note or concern, he relaxes...a smidgen. Ready to be in the moment, he joins with them in the human art of catching up.

At this moment, nothing else matters. Both Charles and Rosa revel in the minutiae, this world that is their favorite escape.

Charles reaches across the table and shakes the bartender's hand as he slides in next to Rosa. She gives him an affectionate squeeze as he does. The bartender, George, smirks and blushes at the affection.

"Hey, George. Good to see ya!" Charles says.

"Thanks! Good to see you also, Charles," George says. "It has been awhile. How goes the fight?"

George, a rare retired Tripper, is a stout black man with a short fro and a long limp; rare, not so much that he survived and retired, but that he elected to stay in this time period, once he was done traveling the worlds. And to be honest, he wasn't in long enough to fully retire. Four years is a full hitch, as far as the PABs are concerned. Although if you get physically or mentally FUBAR'd like George did, they will allow medical retirement. Still for some reason, most of the other twelve retirees went back to the time from whence they came, never to be seen or heard from again.

All three sitting at the table know they are not able to talk about day jobs in detail. The banter quickly moves on to craziness with bar customers. Rosa and Charles both love the way he tells stories and both go silent in order to listen to the latest drunken wisdom story. An oxymoron in its truest form.

CHAPTER SEVEN

John lays around his small and basic apartment. Simply furnished with nondescript items that are hard to see due to the amount of stuff piled on them. The apartment smells like a bachelor blend of stale sweat, food, and stagnant air.

Thank the gods! John has his balcony door open which is letting in the fresh air smell, and the bit of freshness that is surely keeping John alive.

Lower in elevation than most, John can hear the din from the commons below; he has his balcony door open for this very purpose. When it is closed, his apartment gives him a dead zone kind of feeling, like hanging out at a funeral home alone at night, eerie and stagnant. Having the door open gives him that hustle and bustle feeling he loves.

Sometimes he even sleeps out on the balcony. He acquired a cot for this very purpose. It took some looking and hunting, but after chatting with some of the maintenance guys one day, he found out they have a few for times when they are sequestered on a job. Locked in and unable to go back to their apartments, they sleep on cots, next to the top secret devices they are working on. Required to be there so no one can sabotage the technology before it is finished, they may spend weeks fitfully sleeping next to their latest fix it project.

He traded an old handheld video game he truly acquired for one of their precious cots. John had found it laying next to the computers back in that old underground bunker facility from his first mission. He saw it there and recognized it instantly. He remembered it from an article he read about classic handhelds and the roots of the gaming industry. Off-white, with the words "MATTEL ELECTRONICS" across the top, it was adorned with an oval screen, green highlights, four orange directional keys, an on/off switch, and not much else. A small speaker and a worn-off blue label adorned the bottom third of the device.

He had flipped on the switch and some dots appeared with one of them flashing, the LEDs face each other nine to one. The flashing light moved by pressing one of the orange buttons; it moved respectively in the direction of the faded arrow painted on the orange plastic. Moving up and down, awakened the other dots, and they started moving towards the flashing one. He pushed the down arrow to escape the approaching flashing lights, and moved it to the right, leaving the screen and re-entering on the left side. When one of the solids touched him, the handheld erupted in noise. He pushed it hard into his lap to squelch the noise. He—remembered looking up-- expecting to catch some hell. No one had noticed, they being focused on their tasks. He had turned it off and stashed it in his Tripper suit in order to figure it out later.

Each time he sleeps on that cot, he is grateful he put the

device in his pocket instead of stashing it in the cases to be retrieved later. In fact, lesson learned: he never saw those cases again; anything he wants to acquire needs to be on his person. A quick learner of systems and how to skirt them, this knowledge naturally piles up in his brain.

Bang, bang, bang. A heavy knock on the door startles John. First time anybody other than June has knocked and that definitely was not her knock.

Adorned in his finest skivvies, he uses the door as a shield when he opens it. The extraneous noise of the hallway filters around the giant figure standing there. It is Grey!

"Um, hello. I wasn't expecting you," John says.

"I know," he replies. "Let me in...."

John pulls the door open more, still using it as a shield until Grey is through. Then he closes it tight. It clicks its reluctant acknowledgement.

Grey looks down at John, "You can put something on if you want. Doesn't matter to me."

"Um, no. I'm good then. This is my most comfortable way to hang out. If you are really good with it, that is?" John inquires.

"Yep, I'm good. I know I am intruding on your down time, so I will get right to it. Mind if I sit?" Grey asks.

"Sure, how about out on the balcony?" John says.

"No, some of this might be confidential. We best stay inside," Grey says.

John walks over and slides the door closed, revealing quiet music that had been overwhelmed by the din outside. Clean and rhythmic, electronic and deep house, it is indicative of John's time period.

John offers Grey a beverage which he takes and holds in

his hand the entire time, only occasionally sipping from the water contained within.

After settling in, Grey says, "You had asked me about going up top with Rosa and Charles. They are both on board with it and so am I. Part of why I put you off is some formalization of rules and your newness to, um, now."

John nods his head.

"You, however, come from a time frame similar to up top, and have shown strength already. I am confident you will be safe there--and actually come back!" Grey smiles at the last part.

A rogue Tripper wandering about the under city, talking about top secret programs would be a tragedy. Especially for that Tripper: he would no doubt be captured and disposed of. Or, if unable to catch him outright and quickly, the PAB's would run a smear campaign, evil enough to awaken said Tripper's ancestors from the dead in retribution.

John smiles at Grey. Awesome, he thinks. Awesome! I get to see how the other half lives.

"Caveats," Grey continues. "You must listen to Rosa and Charles. Think of it as a mission, of sorts. They are the seniors and they will help you survive the world above."

John laughs!

"I say this is no joke, John. I am confident in your ability to adapt, but if they find out you used to be one from up top, they may just try to take you out. Here the PAB's are not looked upon all that greatly in the deep dark underbelly of the city, or most cities up top from what I hear. I say this because the world you and I live in down here is different.

"Now I have to admit, this is based on learned knowledge and not personal experience. I don't go up top, have no reason to when we are here," Grey says.

"I hear you haven't been above for longer than the 30 years I've been around," John says.

"Pretty accurate," Grey answers. "Not my thing. I am perfectly content down below when we're not working."

"Yeah, but how do you get laid?" John asks him with a smirk.

Smiling, "Easy, there are ways and methods, whenever there is a facility like this and of this size, anywhere in human history, there is a way. They are carded and med checked regularly for safety. I can help you with that if you want, John."

"Really?! I appreciate that. Surprised, but appreciate it just the same!" John replies.

"Ha ha. I know right. It's time to change your mindset. You are a Tripper now, so it's time to start thinking like one. We can do anything, at any time. We are the long range reconnaissance patrols of our time. Well, this time, which is now 'our time.' You have all that it takes except the experienced mindset. I am confident that will come to you soon," Grey states.

"Thank you, Mr. Grey," John says.

"You have the makings of a great Tripper, John," Grey says.

John blushes. Positive reinforcement. What is that? He likes it--whatever it is. He is kind of learning to dish it out. After experiencing it and the feeling it gave him, he tried it out experimentally on a few people. Mildred at the lunch counter blushed brighter than her tomato soup. The guy who sweeps the hall smiled and nodded when John told him how much of a difference a clean floor made. The technicians just looked down at the floor and smiled. No one ever thanks them for anything.

'Hmm, I wonder what kind of response I would get from Mac the Jock if I gave her some?' John thinks.

"So what do you think? Still want to go up top?" Grey asks, removing John from his personal thoughts.

"Yes, definitely. I look forward to it," John says. "And just as a reminder, the revolution I joined back in the day was for the unchosen ones: I have an affinity in my heart for them. Badassery is my term for those in that revolution--with the technology that the uppers had, and the simplistic way we went about wreaking havoc on what you now call the PAB's. They were so reliant on technology, that messing with it became our biggest warrior in the fight. Cool thing was, hardly anybody died that way," John says.

"Just when they found you guys and tried the slaughter thing," Grey says.

"Exactly, but that was the PAB's, not us, wasn't it!" John replies.

Grey gets up, "Like I said, John, you will do well here if you want. I like what you bring to the table and am glad you are on my team. We will work on progressing you quickly." Holding the glass out, he asks, "Kitchen?"

"I'll take it. I'm obsessive about cleaning dishes instantly. " John grabs for the glass.

Both hold it for an instant. "Oh, and wait till you are ready to go for Mackenzie. If you fuck it up, you will pay for it the most," Grey says.

John, turns a little ashen, "You mean, because of what she told us?"

"Not what I meant, and that's a question for her by the way, when you are ready. I mean if you go hard charging or just want to get laid. Like I said there are other, classic means for that. If you want a relationship with a team member, take it extremely slowly. My Trippers are my family and I take it very personally when they fuck with each other—literally or figuratively," Grey says, making intense eye contact with John.

John nods his head and pulls on the glass.

"I get it. Message received loud and clear," he says.

Grey lets go so John can take it, "Get me a pen if you would, I want to write a number down for you. They have something for everyone. Just ask--and tell them you are a Tripper. They will accommodate you and give you a discount even; membership has its privileges, after all."

Grey grabs the provided pen and paper. It took John awhile when he first arrived to figure out what they were. It was part of his integration training. His time had no hand writing devises, no hand anything. It was all automated and digital. No pen, paper, or live painting, anything!

Grey hands the pad and pen back to John. As he heads for the door, he says, "Enjoy! I will see you tomorrow, usual time. When we get back from this trip, you can go up top with Charles and Rosa. I can't wait to hear all about it." As he opens the door to the hall, the noise rolls into the apartment like a tidal wave, but it ends as soon as Grey closes the door behind him.

John walks over to the balcony slider and opens it. The noise returns. Glass in hand, he walks to the kitchen to handle it, and then calls the number. No time like the present. It rings once and a pleasant sultry voice answers, "Yes?"

"Yes, Ma'am, I am looking to touch base with Samantha," he says, reading the name on the pad.

"You might have. Who referred you?" The voice is sultry...and demanding.

"Grey, he's my boss, Ma'am," John says.

"Oh." Her voice is softer this time. "Perfect. Hold one moment, please. We will get you your pleasure shortly. One moment." John is put on hold. He wonders to himself, "What is my pleasure today. Humm...."

A click announces the speaker's arrival to the conversation. "Hello, John, how are you?" This is a new voice--an authoritative yet sultry voice.

"Working on it, Ma'am. Getting better and better!" he says.

"That's 'Madam Samantha,' John. Let's cut to the chase," she says.

"Yes, Madam," John pauses. "I like a woman who can put me in my place." There is a glisten in his eyes.

"Now we are getting somewhere," she says, "Good boy."

CHAPTER EIGHT

John walks into the cafeteria, a gleam in his eye and a bounce in his step. He has gotten laid and it is obvious as hell. Grey is probably the only one that knows how, but everyone notices.

Charles looks at him knowing the look of contentment on his face combined with a cheesy grin, says that he got exactly what he wanted and that is usually only when paid for by an assertive individual. Besides, how else would John get laid? Having watched and participated in enough of that type of activity in the past, he is pretty sure in fact. Note to self: weakness number one. Filed.

John grabs a tray and fills it with all the goodies. Still getting used to solid foods, he decides to grab a little of everything. He does this every time he comes down here to eat. More often than not he eats his meals in his apartment or the commons. Since this, however, is the last meal before mission, he will always eat with his team—per a voiced requirement by Grey.

"I'll take a little of everything today, Mildred," John says.

She smiles at him. She thinks he is cute and assertive,

and likes that in a man. Mildred piles a sample serving of everything, knowing he will return for the things he likes. Today is a brunch-like combination of turkey & gravy with mashed potatoes and something affectionately known as S.O.S. She also adds a scoop of fruit blend and mixed vegetables to balance out the meal.

"Thanks, Lovely," John says to her. "What else you got?"

"Just me, honey... well, and some black pudding," Mildred says as she turns seductively.

John makes direct eye contact with her, "Mildred, you know you melt my butter. But alas, I am off to parts unknown and will have to take a rain check on you, my dear," he says with a tinge of regret.

She puts some black pudding on the tray and hands it to him. He takes it and winks, "Thanks, my darling."

Turning, he faces the grossly empty room, normally full of everyone, feeling like being around other people. This place and the commons are the only large mingle zones in the entire facility.

Only John and the other six members of his team are present at the moment. Not even other Tripper teams are allowed here during pre-meal. In fact, most Tripper teams don't interact at all. Kept separate by design and opposite travel schedules, it is common for two different Tripper teams to never know of the other's existence.

John sidles over to his usual spot between Miokel and June. they always sit in the same positions as if they were in their ready room. The team members--being creatures of habit in the ways that are allowed--compensate for the ever-changing chaos of their day jobs.

"What's up, guys?" John asks jovially as he sits down.

Rosa responds first, "What's up?! Did you visit the

1980's without me?"

John is euphoric. Rosa sees he is glowing. What the hell has he been up to?

"I met someone. She taught me a new phrase and I like it. What's up?" John says, as he raises his chin.

"Oh, that's obnoxious!" Mackenzie responds.

"Exactly!" John says.

Miokel shakes his head and elbows John playfully, "Just what you need: more tools to be obnoxious."

John asks, "Can you have too many tools?"

"No, no you can't," Miokel says.

Everyone goes silent, the nervous pre-mission energy dispersing a bit. This will only be the second time this team as tripped together. The last time was pretty much a cake walk. One could argue the Mackenzie and Miokel being captured almost seemed like part of the plan. Excepting her broken hand, one could easily say Miokel and Mackenzie had their way with those two guards. Other than that, it all went as planned.

Let's see what this one brings.

After about 20 minutes, all are finished. Repeat trips to gather more food and flirt with Mildred have occurred by most; well, the food part at least.

Grey looks at his invisible watch, "OK, tram-ride in 20. See you in ten minutes at the ready room."

He walks off.

The rest of the team does their thing because the boss is not there: they grab-ass and hang out until it is time to go.

CHAPTER NINE

Lee Batard stands on the very bow of the boat, looking out ahead. There is nothing in particular he is looking for; he is enjoying the views of the Mediterranean ahead of the steamer. Having never been this far from shore, he is taking full advantage of all it has to offer. Other than being born for it, one of the reasons he agreed to this job is the opportunity to see and do things he wouldn't normally get to, especially in this time of war. How many people can freely travel the Mediterranean without the strong risk of being accosted? Such is the story he is telling himself as he stands proud and tall at the very tip of the bow. He is not as pretentious and unwise as to put a foot up on the side, and yet, when the captain watches from the sanctity of his bridge, he cannot help but notice the pompous ass standing at the front of his steamer. Perhaps they will get lucky and a big wave will come up and wash him into the sea; then he and his crew would get to keep the woman to themselves.

Mistreated and malnourished, the woman is currently being nursed to health down below in the galley by the cook; his chicken stew is legendary for bringing all but the worst of sicknesses and illnesses to their knees. It will be a short time before his magic brew brings the life back into her eyes.

Based on a conversation the spy and the captain had just before departure, it is the spy's intention to bring this woman back to health. Perhaps even clean her up during the journey by unceremoniously dunking her overboard before reaching their port located on the southeast corner of the Mediterranean Sea. Once there, he will use her, and then bring her back to the boat in order to return her to France for her execution.

The captain is charged with waiting in port for their return. A big fan of being on retainer, he had negotiated this before their departure. He and his crew will be paid to wait, paid to fix their ship and drink. Not too shabby.

CHAPTER TEN

John and Charles walk at a leisurely pace. There is no reason to hurry since it's a short walk. The rest of the team has prep work to do, and no one is making the next trip until tomorrow. Apparently on a multi-jump trip, there is a mandatory wait period between jumps.

John, being into the geekier side of things, is enthralled with the technical aspects of how they travel through time. Nobody else on the team seems to be, which makes it hard for him to gain any technical information.

John did spend time walking around and socializing during his five days off, trying to make connections with Technicians and others in the know. He asked a multitude of questions as to the workings of the machine, the philosophy, and the science behind it that make it work. With everyone being under the rules of no talking and keeping everything top secret to everybody else, it is really tough to make connections with people who are willing to talk to him about it. Every time he broached the subject, they would shutdown. He didn't even get to the questions about the details of how the machine works. Way before that, as soon as he asked what they do here, they shutdown. Sometimes they even walked away. It seems that natural conversation starter from his time frame is taboo in Tripper land. He will have to be patient and find out this stuff over time. It's the kind of stuff he just wants to know--he is passionate about it. The team even teases him about it: his seemingly inappropriate relationship with computers and technology.

Charles talks as he walks, "The surgery was quick and painless. No more heal time than a deep cut and no medical attention needed other than the modern form of a Band-Aid. It took them about five minutes to place the nano-chip and wire it into my voice box system, as I will call it. I'm not into all this 'techno-mumbo-jumbo' as you are, so you will have to ask them when you go to have one put it in. Maybe they will tell you. Who knows?" Charles shrugs his shoulders; he is perfectly ok with not knowing the details of how everything works. He isn't into technology at all, more into the human side of things. One of the reasons he is really intuitive about the people in his work; an absolute reason why he was a successful hit-man as well. He always seems to know what a person is going to do next. This is key in staying one step ahead in his plans for them.

"It has what I call a magnet that is placed under the skin. This magnet hooks in to the magnetic field of our Tripper suit and the brain therein. This way, there is no wireless communication back and forth between the chip and our suit's brain." John is acutely aware of what can be grabbed out of the air without someone's permission. He used to make a living off of it.

Charles looks at John, "If you ever get smart and start

designing these things," he pulls at his Tripper suit with his hands, "Keep that in mind, will you? No wireless. Hardwire or magnetic metallic only. This way, we can use it everywhere we go, unlike the damn comms."

John jumps in, "Yah, I hate that too. It would seem in this day and age, or that one (he points behind him, trying to reference 2114, not whenever they were now), they would have figured something like that out by now. It's just a great example of security not being able to keep up with technology."

Charles is lost in his story at this point, "Where was I?" he asks.

John answers, "Magnets to the suits so we can always use them."

"Ah, yes! Somehow the system hears the language that is spoken around us and tailors our speech as it listens. It is very strange to think in English and hear my voice speaking something entirely different. It takes lots of practice and a while to get used to it!" Charles says.

"What about the other way?" John asks.

"Do you mean, how do I understand what they are saying?"

"Yes," John says.

"That's a little tougher for me, so let me know when you hear a good answer. I know you will be able to translate it into layman terms for me," Charles says. "But, it has something to do with using the body's electrical system to move the sound information from the ears to the nano chip and back to the brain.

That's more than I know I knew." Charles says.

John is intrigued. But with the sealed lips of everyone around the facility, it will take some time to figure it all out. Maybe he will look for those scientists they brought back from here last week and see if he can get in with them on the ground floor in order to gain information from them over time. Besides those three were really cool, what was it they said about fear?

Lost in thought, they walked the rest of the way in silence, up to and including entering the local café they are now sitting in. Knowing they are going to sit and wait for the vans arrival, even that conversation was unnecessary. Both Charles and John are content to contemplate for awhile. John is solving the mysteries of how the machine works, and Charles is thinking about that lovely woman he gets to play with and what Grey told him about the next part of the mission. He is glad he gets to play the protector role with June. It is one he is good at and enjoys.

*****

Charles and John spot the Zuk van on the town's main drag, sitting in front of the shops. Strangely, John recognizes the van. At least that's what his brain tells him, but how could he? He hasn't been here before, right?

Looking over at Charles, John says, "Ok, let me in on it."

Charles looks at him questioningly, a cheesy smirk on his face, eyes a smiling! Unable to contain himself, Charles breaks out in a big grin.

"It is the same van!" John exclaims.

Though Charles' smile progresses into a laugh, he is still not talking.

John is confused, and asks, "How is that possible?"

"Get used to it."

"Used to what?" John is getting angry now. Charles is messing with him and he doesn't like it.

"Paradoxes," is Charles' only answer.

"You mean to tell me, this is the van we used on the last mission? You and I are here to steal this van and leave it so we can use it on the mission we returned from a week ago?" John is starting to love the idea of what is being presented to him in this moment.

John's new job is to travel through time and change things. He has no idea if it is for the greater good or bad. He does know it is not for evil--he would've felt that already. He doesn't know if it is for the people or the money mongers though. Currently, he doesn't care. Don't think he is evil or mean, just that he doesn't really care at the moment. If it doesn't directly involve John, why does it matter? He is as narcissistic as they come and in total denial of this fact. It might explain his confusion as to why the women don't drool at his feet--like he knows they should. He isn't worried: some day they will figure out the error of their ways and make up for lost time.

Charles' voice brings him back to the present moment. "We're not going to steal it; we are going to buy it. No stealing from the public in general." Charles is wagging his finger at John, like he is being naughty.

"You mean we can blow up secret lair farm houses at will, but no stealing bubble gum from the locals?" John asks.

"Not at will, John." Charles says. "We have strict rules and guidelines. You know this, man. You read the manual, passed the exam, all that good stuff. You just chose not to remember them-- the rules that is." Charles is back to the big smile.

John says, "Not that there is anything wrong with that, and this coming from the hitman, by the way!" He laughs. "OK, what are we going to do then?"

"We are going to buy it. It's for sale. Gonna give them a good deal too," Charles smiles again, seems he is having a good time on this quick mission with John—even having fun with John. He is a good guy to hang with; besides it is fun to watch him attempt to pick up most of the females he sees. It doesn't seem to matter if they are young or old, skinny or curvy, John hits on them all. Well, everyone that appears single—apparently, he does seem to have some semblance of boundaries. It's probably because he's had his ass beat too many times. Although any guy who sees John as a threat is insecure as hell in Charles' mind.

The waitress approaches. There was no show to be seen here: John had already attempted hitting on her and even with the language barrier, she shot him down in half a heartbeat.

John sits in amazement while Charles handles the bill with the waitress. It is really cool to hear Charles speaking what comes across to John as perfect dialect of the local version of the Russian language.

*****

Listening to Charles communicate with the waitress, John wonders how he can mess with someone whose voice is saying something different than what the brain is telling it to say. Charles seems to be able to speak interchangeably,

English to Russian and Russian to English.

John loves that after he survives the probationary period, he is eligible to be implanted with said device. Oh man! He can hardly wait! He knows that if he had the chip implant now, he would've been able to pick up the waitress. She just didn't understand what he was saying about how awesome they would be together. He knows she feels it too. John knows she does; she just doesn't want to risk embarrassment by coming on to him. He even tried to get Charles to translate for him, but Charles just sat back in his chair, laughed and waved his hand in front of him as a big "No" while shaking his head.

No translation needed there.

With the meal finished and paid for, Charles and John walk out from the café, stomachs full and happy at the opportunity for ethnic food.

They head over to the van to figure out how obtain it. Luckily, the owner is making his way to the Zuk van with some purchases when they approach. Quickly and efficiently, Charles negotiates with the man. Reaching into his pocket, he pulls out the local currency and doles out the appropriate amount to the now previous van owner.

John can't help but wonder if Charles has a money changer installed in his pocket for just these occasions or if this was another of those weird paradoxical things where the PAB's already know the outcome of Charles' and the Zuk van owner's conversation, and made sure he had enough currency.

The senior Trippers are right, thinking about this stuff too much will drive you crazy. Best not to think about it. . .yeah right, they don't know John very well, do they! Or perhaps they do and that is why they say it. More than likely, it's because they have been through similar processes before, and have learned the hard way themselves. Except maybe Grey, he seems to thrive on not thinking about that stuff. He loves being in that mission's moment!

Charles starts helping the guy with his belongings. Deciding John has been lost in space long enough, he nudges him and gets him to help remove anything the guy wants from the van. The previous owner looks at John, smiles big and nods to him repeatedly. Not knowing that Charles has just told the guy John is an upcoming movie star from the country of America, he has no idea why he is gaining so much respect. He simply smiles and nods back.

Leaving the guy smiling, waving, and standing amongst his stuff as they pull off in the Zuk van that was his until a couple moments ago, they head out of town in the direction they walked in from.

CHAPTER ELEVEN

Charles pulls up in front of one of the barns. Having just arrived from purchasing the van, he and John are stashing it for later use--although to them, this was last week.

John jumps out of the passenger's side and saunters up to the sliding doors. His style of walk--a byproduct of his build rather than his unrelenting desire to be John Wayne--he moves as though he is a little winded at all times. It has been six months (more than that actually) since he started training to be a Tripper. His previous almost 30 years were spent in the year 2054 and earlier. Almost all of those years were spent living a sedentary lifestyle, as did most people in his class.

John grew up in a world full of computers and processed items. Food was in pill form, specially made and formulated from a computer generated list of his body's needs. His body was checked by the house management system each and every night while he slept. Each housing unit had its own management system; each house's system was plugged in the central system. All needed items were delivered automatically as the resident consumed them; trash was emptied automatically and what few consumables the house contained were replaced as used. No physical effort at all was required to maintain that type of housing unit. Dusting, washing, and bed making all happened autonomously while he was gone from his residence.

In Tripper school, while learning about the Earth's human time line, the trainers referred to his time frame as "Wall-E-World," a derivative from an early 2000's movie about humans being turned into gelatin due to lack of activity. In class, he also learned that in 2114, the other half of 2000's mid-century picture is still being suppressed.

With everything being automated in John's time frame, there was a lot less need for workers and producers. Computers, robots, and machines were so well made, they seemed to last forever. With built-in maintenance, development systems, and automatic delivery of replacement parts or consumables which were all produced by machines, there was very little for human beings to actually do. This left billions of humans with literally no useful purpose.

The computers of the time got on the problem because it was up to them to come up with a solution. There were nearly 8 1/2 billion people on the planet, and only about 4 billion humans were needed to create a sustainable commerce and a never ending living system. NELS is the acronym the computer brains came up with to call their management plan. All human history, the Earth's cycles, human nature and the rest of the Earth's natural cycle were taken into account. Within a radically short time frame of ten years, 4 billion humans were removed from the old system and deposited into a new sustainable NELS environment. It was done so quickly and efficiently that almost all were oblivious to the fact that half the world's population was not in the new system. It was only after a few years of using the new system that some of the remaining 4 Billion became aware of the computer's method of balancing the human population.

A majority of the other 4 billion humans were either shut-off and locked up in high-density areas where they already lived or were relocated there, in order to build density; before walling these areas off and removing almost all resources needed to survive.

Within a quick, brutal 20 years, the bad parts of human nature thinned the unwanted half of the human race to a mere 400 million. It was somewhere amidst that extreme population reduction that some of the unchosen woke up and realized they had been placed in an environment intended to destroy them. It was then that they started their war against NELS.

They managed to penetrate the system undetected at times, and would wreak havoc on the computer's version of Utopia. The 20 years of absolute chaos had weeded out the weakest, and least competent of the lot, leaving the most determined, brightest and fiercest humans alive. This forced survival of the fittest, result to the computer system's plan, was a human-like error indeed and resulted in the creation a super force of angry humans.

John quickly learned about this underground super force, through the social media system. The social media apps and system moved at such speed, that even the computers couldn't filter out the data fast enough. Human nature's curiosity and instant access to the world's information created a viral firestorm of information about this unplanned result to the bigger plan of reducing the earth's human population.

In 2054, the baby production was nearly nil. Occasionally one was brought up to fill a gap, mostly the humans fortunate enough to be living John's lifestyle, were populated by the occasional oops in birth control. At 0.001% risk of birth control failure, it would still be approximately 100 years before the system would need to remove birth control from their human's sustenance pills. Yet, way before reaching that stage, something happened.

Most would call it revolution.

That revolution and his boredom, are the reasons John is standing here today sliding open an old barn door, produced in an era of Communist reign and from a time frame before he even existed, or the craziness described above even happened.

CHAPTER TWELVE

When John returns from the Zuk van retrieval, Miokel grabs him and Mackenzie. They move out under the neglected apple orchard to sit.

The weather outside is nearly exact to what it was when they were here a week ago; shining sun, cool fall breeze blowing, dry leaves about the area and a smell of overly ripe apples and rotten leaves fills the air between breezes. The same insects fly by, preparing themselves for winter or their death, ensuring first, the next generation's existence.

Miokel grabs a seat on the ground, careful not to sit on any decaying apples or dying bugs and leans his back to one of the tree trunks; Mackenzie and John do the same.

"The three of us will be teamed up together on this one," Miokel says, "We get to do some good tom foolery against a bastard of a man. A man who, and it said this in his file, 'would trade his mother for a secret'. After reading his entire file, I have no doubt this is true. That is why it will feel really awesome when we see this come into fruition. We are going to set him up as the fall guy, he deserves it and it's going to be great to relieve history of a man such as this."

"Wow!" John says, "You really don't like this guy."

"I don't, I really don't," Miokel says, "It's the unfair and totally awesome ability to open a file, and read what has already occurred in his life, that set him up for the fall. He is a dingus of the greatest kind. His name literally means 'the bastard'."

John laughs!

"For reals?" Mackenzie says.

"Yes, for reals. He chose to live a life that lived up to and, I would say, surpassed the expectations of his name.

At the same time, hopefully, we will save a life." He adds.

"We are going to save someone this time?" Mac asks.

"Perhaps," Miokel replies.

She asks, "What do you mean, perhaps?"

"Well, we are going to give them a chance, it is still up to them and their free will. She will have to choose a different path."

"What, we can't yet influence people's minds!" John pauses to do some thinking, "At least not to that degree." John says.

Miokel looks at him questioningly.

"Well, I just happen to know they were working on it in my time. Knew for a fact, not that I had anything to do with it." John says.

"Then why are you blushing!" Mackenzie calls him out, laughing.

Smiling, Miokel says, "Perhaps that went by the wayside, just like those food pills you all use to eat."

"Haha" John mocks. "Seriously, though, what did happen to the food pills and everything else for that matter?"

Getting no response, he addresses Miokel directly. "Seriously, do you know what has happened between then and now? I mean our now, not now, now!" John in his anger manages to keep a straight face at that statement.

Miokel blesses him with his best answer, "I don't know for sure yet. I have a great theory working actually. It's how I occupy myself while we are not working. I am into history, so you can image how this job feeds that fuel! The last trip we took actually helped fill in a lot of the holes in my theories."

John and Mackenzie look at him in amazement. They will get to know him a lot better on this trip, they think.

"Ok, back on the topic at hand," Miokel says, "We have two things to accomplish; one will wait until the very end, the other we will get to work on asap. First and foremost we have to convince the Armenian's French foreign legion troops that Lee Batard is a double agent and not who he seems. Which, with who he is personality wise, should not be too hard. And also to take the woman I mentioned, back to prison where she can be tried and guillotined for her crimes against..."

"I thought we were going to save her?" John asks.

"Perhaps, it is someone else we are saving," Mackenzie says.

Miokel raises and lowers his eyebrows mischievously.

"Perhaps yes to both." He says.

"Since I am the only one with a translator chip installed, I will do all the talking. Chances are, none of the Armenians speak English, maybe a random one or two, so be careful what you say around others, be smart and think! We are the strangers there, and we stand out.

Although you two will become more and more comfortable with our travels; we will more often than not, come across as completely strange. Obvious even with our attire, that we are not local. Especially when we are surrounded by Ottomans, Armenians, and other totally non-futuristic peoples.

So you two will be presented by me as agents from America, here to help the cause. Best I can do since neither of you have anything close to resembling a British accent."

"What cause?" Mackenzie says.

"What cause depends on who we are talking to. . .just be prepared for anything. Good things to know: this is early in 1917 and the Americans have yet to enter WW1, so you guys can play up the shhh factor of you not really being here. Use that to derail any questions a rare English speaker may have for you as to your background. Just be secretive."

"As a spy would be." John adds.

"Yes, but be careful about representing yourself as a spy, to anybody or in your mind." Miokel says.

"...Because spies very rarely have happy endings." John interrupts.

Miokel says, "Exactly, based on history, their stories generally end in death."

"And based on what you said, here's hoping this guy's ends in death." John says.

"I'm not one for wishing death on anybody. It sounds like this guy deserves it, though; anyone who would sell his mother for a secret has just desserts coming to him." Mackenzie says.

The three team members sitting under the trees continue to plot and scheme way longer than necessary.

Perhaps it is the fresh air and ambiance. Spending most of their time under the surface of the earth, breathing the same air over and over has its negative effects on the human psyche. The smells of fresh air, dirt and fruit rejuvenate, conscious of that fact or not.

To someone like John, who has spent most of his life literally living in a bubble, it has awakening effects on his body. He feels like he has never felt before. He thinks it is because of his new found love, his job. Perhaps that is some of it, his body does celebrate his joy, and it also celebrates the scents and feeling of fresh air. It is indescribable what a little nature time does for him. If his body were forced to, it would say: the ambiance of the air that has been continually spinning its way across the lands and oceans of the earth is full of the world's essence and can only be felt and experienced by drawing it into his lungs. His lungs yearn to experience all the air the earth has to offer. The ocean scents, the desert's dryness, and the mountain's crispness; they each bring different scents. The intermingling of seaweed, fish poop and salt in the ocean's air that makes the nose grimace at times. The body moisture sucking dryness of the super-heated and dust filled, putrid scents of the desert's absence of green growth, yet filled with the multitude of scents the sands bring to it. Not to mention the nostril freezing, blaring cold scents of the mountains air, filled with the scents of the below and the above, as the howling wind works its way from the lowlands to the sky touching altitudes of the mountains. The frozen snow mingles with the earthy smell of the desert's thousand types of minerals that make up its sands, finally intertwining with the rotting organic matter of the seas to create a fantastical blend of genuine earth.

John's body rejoices as he sits and contemplates who will die, who will get hurt and who will just plain ole drop the ball on this mission. The fresh air helps him know it will not be him. It will be somebody else; it will be the other guys and not his Tripper team. Or Mr. Grey's team for that matter, as it is really his and Miokel's team. As his brain worries semantics, John knows they are in it together and always will be. He has finally found his purpose and place. His body rejoices in that as well.

CHAPTER THIRTEEN

The team gathers back up inside the now familiar cold war era farm shed. With a little more than an hour to wait before their next jump through time, Grey figures this is a safe place to wait it out and force some team down time.

Grey sizes them up and sees that they are good to go, all seem prepared and physically ready. He goes through his mental checklist and finds one box unchecked. He has missed something.

"One more thing to cover before our next tram ride," Grey says, "Comms will be available for use on the next part of the mission. In the year 1917, there is no technology existing that can hear or sense our level of communications. What I mean by that is radio communications are very primitive right now. I don't know if you know your history, but a huge part of the world is involved in what they call WW1, Ring any bells?"

Nods all around.

Grey continues, "Right now there is some poor SOB in a hot air balloon, tethered by a rope to the ground on his side of the line, floating high above the battlefield trying to radio down to those that need to know what is going on, on the other side of the line before someone gets a lucky shot off at the balloon, exploding the gases held within and sending them on a quick, flame-filled decent to their death."

Rosa pipes in, "Damn, that's gotta be a bad way to go." Mackenzie nods her head in agreement, and says, "I know right!"

Smiling at their perspective Grey goes on, "Radio technology is so new that it is easily controlled. The governments of the world; remember in this time the world is not united."

June interrupts, "The world is united! What does that mean," looking over at John, "Did they tell us that in training?"

John, "No hon, they just assumed everyone knows I guess, they weren't thinking when you are from." He winks at her.

"Can we hold that line of history, for now, June? We need to stay focused." Grey asks of her in his usual boss way of saying, not now.

"Yes, sorry." She puts her head down.

"No apology needed, it is a good reminder of the different world you are from." Grey smiles at her and continues, "Only countries with more advanced technology have the ability to produce the radios and they have banned their use by civilians for security reasons and to prevent them from hearing what is going on in detail. Strange enough, most news is spread by the newspaper at this point. I say that because myself, Miokel, and John had never seen or used paper before becoming trippers. June, you may be the only one here who didn't know that somewhere in time it was no longer produced. Do you know John?"

"2024 I believe it was, after the paper wars." John replies.

Charles shows us he is still awake, "They fought over paper? Like there was none left?" he asks.

John answers, "No they fought over the production of paper and the land needed to produce it. The short answer would be: too many humans, not enough space, they were fighting over space priority. The areas that trees grow the best are also most conducive to human living as well. It is good to note, though, that the 'paper war' as it was called was not a battlefield war like the world war Grey is talking about. It was a war of espionage and spies, within the corporations and governments of the paper producing countries. The first of its kind as far as I know; before this one, wars, even the cold war of the 70's & 80's were between different countries. This war was between the corporations and the governments of several countries. The governments teamed up together against the money and power of the corporations. In that time companies had more money to work with than the governments and were in the beginnings of ruling the world through similar tactics used by government organisations of the past, the past to me that is."

June, "What does that mean exactly? I'm trying to keep up, but it all sounds like hogwash to me!" June feels so innocent and naive, more than usual with her ignorance of history. Perhaps she should let herself off the hook since it happened long after she would have been dead.

At this point the quiet one, Miokel pipes in, "I wouldn't take it personally June, none of this was on the human mind at the time. In your time, it was governments making all the decisions and in our time," he points to John and Grey, "The corporations, what we all now call the PAB's or the Powers that Be are running the world. It's no longer about Democrat, Republican, Monarchy or Communism; all have succumbed to the power of Commercialism. The whole world has!"

John adds, "Well the money part of it - follow the money right! Always follow the money, it will tell you the purpose of it all. As I see it, the governments were persuaded to take fewer and fewer taxes from the corporations and more and more from their citizens, and over time the citizens had less money to give the governments and the corporations gained a larger percentage of the world's monies and valuables; enabling them to unite the world through commerce and commercialism. Pretty soon the governments of the various countries had no pull or power at all."

Grey says, "And that's when it all changed, the whole world became about profit margins and producing consumables, to get the money the corporations were paying their employees and back into the hands of the companies that paid them. Eventually, the corporations grew into massive entities that formed a coalition they so humbly call the PAB's, as Miokel stated. The committee of 12 companies is who pays our salary and sends us on these missions. The world is no longer run by the governments as some of you knew them, they no longer exist; ancient and archaic dinosaurs, they now only exist in history, and currently as names on a map. The United States is a land mass area, as is Russia, India and any other former country. The PAB's have reorganized the world into economic producing areas."

John interrupts, "How so? Like at the source of the supplies? Or what, because in my time there were the chosen and the revolutionaries trying to upset the balance, although maybe the companies were truly in charge then also, just closeted and behind the scenes still. I don't remember much talk of governments; come to think of it, it was about whom you worked for and what you produced!"

Rosa says, "Grey wouldn't know, he hasn't been up top in 70 years!"

Most of the team laughs at this. John, Mackenzie and June still new to the whole concept just look confused, although John seems to get it somewhat; maybe because he is from a little closer in time to what they are talking about than the other two rookies. Rosa and Charles have had a couple years to understand the concepts in their brains. June and Mackenzie's brains are new to the concept of corporations openly running the world; and even further, June only knows corporations as a relatively new concept. Albeit a concept she knows is improving lives and giving people she knows a sustainable income, allowing them to buy cars and houses. Not to mention extra money for her and her friends to grift.

Grey, waving his hand around in frustration, interrupts, "Ok, okay, O-KAY ... enough. This is supposed to be a brief on the next part of the mission, not a lesson in history. This is not the time and place!"

His team goes silent.

After a moment, Grey attempts to continue with their purpose, "Where was I? Anybody?"

Miokel helps him out, "Radio balloon men being shot down in a blaze of glory for their cause."

"Thanks. Radio communication currently, mostly exists in Europe for the war, and to communicate back and forth to the governments from the war. Where we are headed, there is next to no possibility for someone to hijack our communications, therefore, this will be half of yours first time using communication devices during a mission. Here's the thing: unless you consciously mute the system everything you say will be communicated to the other six. Everything. . .every swear word, catcall and sneeze will be sent over the comms. The unless part comes from a mute button of sorts, just remember you have to engage and disengage the mute."

John says, "Wait, except it's not really a button, it's my brain imagining the button being pushed and pushed again."

Grey replies, "If that works for you, yes. For me, it's a switch imaged in my brain. I'm sure it's different for each. If you are having a difficult time creating an on and off, let me know, and I or someone else will help you out."

Charles pipes in finally, "How will we know if John's mute is actually working or not?" He and Rosa start laughing hysterically and even John has to admit it was funny and true.

"Only time will tell." Grey laughs out in response.

"Ok, we are obviously punchy today and unfocused; let's get focused and stay safe. Remember we are not at home in our comfort zone." He says.

Charles says, "I'm in my comfort zone."

"Yes." Grey has to admit, "Yet, we are not home. Let's remember we are on mission and anything can happen. So let me get this out before I forget to tell you three: if we think someone is or may be able to listen to us we will have to go dark or in other words, stop using the comms and regroup. You guys remember your training on that?" they all nod in confirmation. "Good, remember the code for going dark is 'big brother hears all.'"

John, "Big brother hears all, got it." The other two just nod again.

"Good, ok. Let's get settled in for the day, tram ride commences at dusk."

CHAPTER FOURTEEN

After having a substantial amount of soup, as much as an ailed body can handle, Mata Hari comes out of the cabin and onto the deck of the steamer.

Breathing deep, she takes in the salty air. A second deep breath brings a sting to her nostrils as the salt penetrates the membranes of her inner sanctum. Her eyes water and her nose fills with runny mucous, as her body's defense mechanisms do their thing. Instead of softening her breath, she takes another long deep breath, reveling in the discomfort that the sea air brings to her being. About a day ago, she was near dead and all hope was lost. There was nothing she could do but remain stubborn until death and not giving them the satisfaction of gaining the knowledge they desire from her.

She thinks what they really want is dirt on, and leverage against, the powerful men she has gained intimate knowledge of. They will use the information against these powerful men, and to aid in France's battle for supremacy against any and all enemies of France, perceived or real.

Feeling the soup and air overwhelm her body, it awakens it. She feels more power; an urge to stand tall has her correcting her posture, leaving the broken being behind. As her eyes come into focus, as the haze leaves them, she notices Lee Batard standing in the bow of the boat, doing his best to represent, whatever it is he is representing.

Ah, if she only had a pistol or rifle, it all would be over so fast.

Even through her deathbed eyes, she tagged him as a fixer when she saw him. She has dealt with his kind before. They are so used to everybody being afraid of them and the best thing to do was to address them directly, express no fear, and see what happens. Just be careful, they will do anything.

Deciding to get this over with, she walks up to him. Before he even turns, she asks her first question.

"So what exactly is it you are asking of me?" Mata Hari says.

Without turning he replies, "You will be required to use your normal methods and wiles to influence an arrogant man named Agha Petros, he will hand over a cache of precious jewels to me. These jewels will be used to finance France, and the bribing of agents against her, in order to help her win the war! I care not how we come to accomplish this goal, just that it will happen."

He turns his head and looks at her.

"The prize and incentive for you is a chance at the abolition of your crimes against France. You will stand tall before the courts and I will attest to your great help in the accomplishment of this goal. They will have no choice but to grant my wish of this, seeing your actions as atonement." Lee Batard says.

She looks at him skeptically, "I am not as confident of

that as are you! I do not have the faith that you have in that." Mata Hari says.

"You must," he says, "I do." He says as he looks away from her.

"Time will tell on that." She says.

"And how will just hanging around with this, what was he name again?" she asks.

"Agha Petros, he is a great man and an influencer to those that know him. He will help our cause." Lee Batard says.

Mata Hari says under her breath, "Our cause...."

"What was that?" Lee Batard says.

She says nothing.

"What was that!" he yells. Lee Batard takes off his hat and smacks her on the head with it several times.

"I'm not sure my cause and yours are the same." She replies finally.

"They are until I say they are not." He says, hitting her several more times with the hat for emphasis.

She cowers for protection, not fear, till he finishes.

She then asks, "What if just being around him isn't enough to convince him to give up the jewels and help France?"

"Well then perhaps you will just have to have intercourse with him then!" Lee Batard answers, "He is a friend of mine and I know this will work. I have used that very tactic with him before, and it has worked every time I've used it! It may even be his preferred method." He winks at her.

Disgusted, she looks at the floorboards, it would not be the first time she slept with someone for personal gain, it has become a habit in fact. She hopes to someday move

on from that.
    First she has to survive the next few days.

CHAPTER FIFTEEN

1917

Mackenzie opens her eyes, blinking them a few times as they come into focus. Her chin is on her chest, her eyes focused on the white powdery ground. This time, she finds herself on her knees, the last jump it was her side, the first one her back. It seems each trip landing will be different. She knows her mind will absorb the data of her landings, and move it into statistical categories automatically. It will keep track and let her know how many times she lands on her knees, back, left or right side.

Statistically, her brain is superior and automatic; one of the strong reasons she was a great professional soccer player. Her brain kept all the data from each game film she watched; every time she played against a team, her mind kept track of what each player did; it learned their tendencies in each situation. She would then use this information to pick them apart strategically, whether through offense or defense.

It was this same statistical analysis that eventually made it impossible to hide from, and lie to herself about her husband's philandering. Where was it though, when he eventually told her the truth after her strategic questioning and she lost all rational thought?

As the static slowly dissipates from her body, the powder releases and floats its way to the ground or upwards into the room's current, depending on its mood. As her awareness comes into focus as well, she realizes they have arrived at their second jump point. Mackenzie is excited about this mission. She will have an opportunity to make up to Miokel, her lack of professionalism on their first mission. He assures her, she did great and has nothing to make up for. She isn't there yet in her mind, and it is important to her. She doesn't let team members down.

She rubs her wrists, looking at the remaining bruises, amazed that the bones in her hand have been healed, but the parts of her that were not treated are still slowly doing their thing. How awesome would it be to put her entire body into one of those magical bandages, healing all her old sports wounds?

*****

Up on their feet and looking around, the team notices they are in an adobe structure, completely and utterly devoid of anything. No furniture, no floor, just the white dust of powdery limestone dirt adorning the walls and nothing else. The only thing they can smell or taste is the dust in the room.

The floors, pounded solid by years of use, are hard as a rock, yet still able to release dust up into the air as the team begins to move around and regain their feet.

No one needs to be resuscitated this time, a big win for

the team. Not a word about that fact is mentioned as they all gather their gear and wits.

There is a heavy wooden door on the north side of the structure and a myriad of sounds work their way quietly inside, in spite of its thickness. Or perhaps the sounds work their way through a few tiny cracks in the just as thick shutters located on the two window openings, located one on each side, left and right of the door. The shudders are the only thing that keeps the outside, outside. No glass windows or remnants of their existence can be seen anywhere in the room. The south side of the room contains another door, just as solid but sans the street sounds of the north door. It is possible this one escapes into a back alley or courtyard.

Rosa finds her way out the south door quickly; once again it is her job to secure their location.

Closing the door tight behind her, she sees she is in a small courtyard surrounded by the same adobe blocks and stucco type finish the building is made of. The walls stand about three meters high and block off the area to prying eyes. Located at the back, the southernmost part of the yard, is a thick wooden gate made of the same materials as the structure's doors. This place is part fortress, heavy duty in construction and built to keep what is outside of the compound, outside. It is so successful that it has managed to keep out everything, the courtyard is as empty as the inside of the building.

Rosa heads to the back gate removes a piece of iron securing the latch and lifts the heavy iron latch. She pulls the gate inward and listens, hearing nothing as she peeks her head out. She sees an alley about two meters wide, flowing east to west. At each end she notices the goings on of the streets, the alley itself seems devoid of all movement. It is, however, full of trash, various forms of other debris and many gates such as the one she is holding on to. She sees about a dozen such gates sandwiched between the ends of the alley.

Closing the gate and turning around, she hears the building's back door open. Reaching for her weapon, she pulls out her favorite pistol, the 1911. Once again, happy to be able to carry it.

The rest of the team is exiting the building and coming in her direction.

"We peaked out front and nothing out of the ordinary is going on there. How about out the back?" Grey says to her.

"I was on it!" she replies, "Why did you do that?"

"No reason to be angry Rosa. The room is empty, and John decided to keep breathing this time, so we had nothing else to do." Grey says.

Rosa relaxes a bit, makes total sense to her.

"The back gate goes into an alley, which ends on two different streets, normal alley junk and trash back there, and from the smell of it, that's where the bathroom is too." She says.

Rosa notices the team all staring at her. Then she sees John starting to laugh while looking at her. Are they messing with her about something?

John notices her dress first, his laugh starts quietly and quickly moves to almost hysterical as he checks her out. He has to admit she looks hot, but he just never thought he would ever get to see her dressed, well in a dress. It's amazing how different she really looks

Looking down, Rosa looks at herself and having never

seen her adult self in a dress, she is as shocked as everybody else; strange indeed. Her tripper suit has switched to some kind of lacy, frilly creation. The lace from the top of the dress trickles down her shoulders and is intermingling with a heavy fabric that goes from there to her ankles. It is then that she notices her high tech featherweight boots made out of the same high tech, bomb proof material as her tripper suit. What normally looks similar to the canvas high tops sneakers of popularity, are currently appearing as fancy, open toed, impractically heeled shoes.

Miokel looks over and sees Rosa standing there. Only her ankles are showing, but damn! That is enough for him. Muscle toned and thin from years of activity, her legs are looking lithe. Moving his eyes up, he sees the dress has a neckline that does come down a bit, exposing her shoulders. Muscles pull seductively at her collar bone.

Realizing he's been caught by Rosa, Miokel blushes instantly.

"Sorry." he says.

"No actually, if it woke you up, I should dress like this more often." She says winking at him.

Miokel laughs, "Maybe you should!"

She wiggles her toes, marveling that she can feel the breeze gently brushing her toe hair and the heat of the sun on the tops of her feet.

After a moment, she wills them to switch themselves into leather walking boots and the breeze disappears from her toes. The dress she can put up with, but impracticality, never.

John is still laughing.

"John, if you don't shut up, I'm going to pummel you!"

she says finally.

Still laughing, "I know, I know, I'm sorry." John replies, "I'm not meaning to pick on you. It's just the look on your face is priceless. I wish we could carry cameras so I could take a picture of it and show you. The look on your face I mean, not the dress." John says.

"If it's any consolation, I would be uncomfortable in one as well." John says and then laughs even harder.

Rosa can't help but laugh either, John's statement is funny! Or maybe it's the strange breeze coming up her legs tickling places that aren't usually graced by nature's currents. Either way, it is what is, and it is not a surprise that her trip-suit has her wearing a dress in 1917. Seems pretty standard in fact.

Suddenly they hear a door slamming shut, bam! Miokel and Rosa go silent, as does the rest of the team. They hear something moving towards them from over the wall and in the yard space next to them. The pads are light on the ground, yet they can tell it is something big, perhaps a couple humans! Grey, Miokel, Rosa and Charles all draw their weapons.

June and John have yet to add a weapon to their tripper suit; while Mackenzie feels around for hers, she knows it is in there somewhere, the non-true appearance of the suit is making it harder.

Meanwhile, the sound gets closer, softly footsteps pad their way closer to the wall that is dividing the team from the being on the other side.

Charles moves towards the wall in a crouch, he decides it is better to be close to the wall in order to surprise the being if it decides to jump the wall. He moves in close, his left side against the wall, crouched and ready to spring into action; he hears the sounds stop as it reaches the wall. He hears a sudden motion and looks up expecting a human to appear before him. Instead, he sees nothing.

Looking over at the team, he sees several of them smiling and a few looks of shock as well. Curious Charles stands up slowly, turning towards the wall as he rises to his full height, weapon pointed at the ready.

What Charles sees does shock him a bit and he startles, taking a step back involuntary. A massive head cocks to the side at his action, curious as to what is going on in the courtyard next to it.

The head is poking over the wall; two paws are on the wall as well. A dark snout and ears accentuate the massive head, the rest of its fur seems to be a tan or cream color.

"Holy shit!" is Charles' truth response.

Closest to the dog, it is obvious to him that the dog is bigger than he is. Even so, it would have to be a giant to be able to stand with its paws on the wall and look over.

"Be careful Charles." Miokel says, "I think it's a sheepdog, a Kangal they are called I believe. It might be protecting something over there."

"It's like nine feet tall!" Charles says.

"Not quite, but they are known to be big. It might be standing on something." Miokel says.

Charles puts his revolver away. The dog cocks his head sideways again. Charles approaches the giant head and the dark eye brows go up as if it is asking "really?"

Slowly Charles moves in. He has to look up at the dog; he reaches up and lets it sniff at his hand. The dog nuzzles against it.

"I think you are good." Miokel says.

Charles starts to scratch and pet the dog, the big dog is

all about it and lets him. He reaches up with the other hand and scratches behind both of his ears.

"It appears our neighbor is friendly." Charles says.

John comes over and says, "I'll take one for the team. Why don't you stand on my back and see what's going on over there." He gets down on all fours next to the wall.

Charles puts a foot on his back and uses it to launch himself up and grabs the top of the 3 meter tall wall with one hand. Pulling himself up, he sits on the wall, while petting the giant friendly dog. It's hard to believe this big bundle of love would hurt anybody, but put him in charge of a herd and that will change. Work is work.

Having a sight and height advantage, Charles utilizes the opportunity to recon his surroundings. Not much can be seen except the far streets at each end of the row of buildings. The tall walls hiding everything but what is in his courtyard and the one the Kangal dog is in.

Looking into the dog's courtyard, he sees it is twice the size of theirs and shows signs of having some kind of livestock in it from time to time. It appears the dog is between gigs, perhaps this is why he is being so friendly. He might be here alone awaiting the arrival of sheep or something along those lines.

Looking straight down, Charles sees that the dog is indeed standing on about a two-foot tall wooden platform, with a straw filled, ancient mattress on top. This must be its living quarters when the yard is full of livestock. The dog is surely taking advantage of the empty house while he can.

Thinking, Charles realizes this is an assumption, and desires to check out the house. He looks in Grey's direction and says, "The house?" pointing at the building next door.

"Maybe later." Grey says, "We have to get moving. There are some time constraints to this mission."

Charles pets the dog a little more, and whispers in his ear, "I will be back later, and will bring you some treats when I find some."

The dog, tongue hanging and tail wagging, smiles at him in agreement.

*****

Charles jumps down from the stucco and block wall. The team as a unit, walk towards the back door of their primitive domicile. Suddenly Gray stops and puts a finger to his ear. He wiggles it around, jams it inside and repeats the process.

June, right next to him, asks "Are you ok? You got a bug in your ear or something?"

"No, worse." He says.

The team stops.

"Worse!" June says.

Grey looks at Miokel, finger still in his ear, "Comms aren't working." he says.

Miokel mirroring Grey, puts a finger in his ear. They stand there for a couple of seconds, wiggling their respective fingers in their ears while looking at each other.

John says, "If I didn't know any better, I'd say you two were aliens communicating with each other, by some strange finger and ear waggling form of telepathy."

"Seriously you two." Charles says, "If they aren't working, they aren't working. You look like a couple of idiots."

Miokel and Grey drop their fingers instantly.

"That's never happened before." Grey says.

"Maybe it's the double jump. They forgot to program them differently for this part." Miokel says.

"When we did test jumps, multiples, the comms always worked fine. Damn it." Grey says.

"Damn it." he says again, "We will have to adapt the plan a little bit. Maybe the technicians will be able to fix it before the end of the mission."

"What does that mean?" John asks. "They are watching us! How?"

Miokel answers, "Kind of. They can see (he uses air quotes) can see results, and what's going on with a long delay. Long being: hours-to-days depending on how far back we are in time. If we are on a short jump, one that is back a few years, they can help us out. Not so sure about this one."

"Wait, are you saying part of this deal is they can control technology in use 100 years in the past, how is that possible?" John says.

"Who cares." Rosa pipes in, "All I know is that's how they get us home too! So I just go with it and don't reason why it to death."

"But it's not logical!" John exclaims

Miokel nudges John, "If you think too much, you're not going to make it. I'm telling ya... gotta open that mind to ANY possibility. Those self-limiting belief systems will just keep you down." He says.

"Great! I've got two of you intellectual warriors to deal with." Rosa says, turning to smile and wink at Charles as well.

John says, "But..."

"Knock it off John!" Grey says. "And open the door."

Unbeknownst to John, he had stopped walking and was blocking the back door, while he tried to induce the logic of it all into the part of his brain that has been taught limitations.

He turns and opens the door, walking through the threshold in a daze; John shakes his head in amazement. He just thought he would travel the world and do cool things, he didn't know he would grow in the process.

Bonus!

Grey and Miokel look at each other with confusion on their faces. Something strange was going on, not John's personal growth, but something else. It is a faint instinctual feeling, back in the subconscious parts of their minds. The seed is just starting to break out of its shell, albeit far below the surface, unseen as to its growth.

As the team members walk inside, the door bangs as the last team member shuts it solid, keeping the dust and wind outside.

The Kangal dog next door raises his head, the noise of the door shutting gaining his attention. Laying on his platform, he scans the empty yard space afore him. The last sheep were taken away a few days ago, it is empty. With them gone and his new neighbors safely inside, there is nothing for him to do but go back to sleep and wait.

CHAPTER SIXTEEN

June spots her as soon as June enters the hotel lobby, sitting in an overstuffed chair and primping her face, she has a presence that is hard to miss. Suddenly feeling like she is being watched, June notices that amongst the other hotel guests, she has a similar presence and is gaining attention as well. Taking this in and feeling the confidence it gives, June covers the distance across the lobby to where Mata Hari is sitting in a chair that is located in a small lounge off to one side of the main lobby.

Mata Hari looks up as June approaches and expresses a look of familiarity towards June. Seems the feeling is mutual, they are cut of the same cloth.

Mata Hari speaks first, "Well, I see I am not the only one this far from home." She says to June in English.

"True, that is." June says. If she only knew how from home she really is.

"What brings you here?" Mata Hari asks.

"Trying to escape the war," after a pause, "But it seems to be following me." June looks at the floor in discomfort. "What about you mi lady, what brings you here?"

Mata Hari looks up from her face mirror, and after

giving her a look, makes up an answer, "I am here to help influence someone, and close a deal." Guess she didn't make it up after all.

"Interesting, we have similar goals." June sits next to her, in another overstuffed chair. "No wonder I felt the need to come introduce myself."

June pulls out her mirror. To Mata Hari, it appears out of nowhere. Not only that, but it is different than any she has seen before. Its gold finish seems ancient and unknown to her. It opens in June's hand with nary a sound. It almost seems to hover above her palm.

Instead of looking into her compact mirror, June is actually looking around. She seeks out Charles and finds him at the hotel desk, checking them in. His back to her, she wonders how to let him know she was in, then she looks above him at the mirror on the wall behind the desk clerk and spots him looking at her. With no acknowledgement, she focuses back on Mata Hari.

"Well, it seems we are about checked in, perhaps I will see you at the ball tomorrow?" June says closing the compact mirror which seems to disappear, rather than being placed in the small purse June is carrying.

June stands.

Glancing up from her mirror, Mata Hari says, "Perhaps we shall see each other again at the ball, have a drink and an actual conversation. Maybe we both will have progress to talk about."

"Perhaps. Good day." June says as she walks away.

Joining Charles and the bellman near the base of the stairs, she takes Charles's offered arm and looks at him. Before she can say anything he speaks, "Don't worry, she's watching us." Grinning he takes the first of the steps towards their room. "Good" June replies, as she lifts her skirt and takes the stairs with him, albeit gracefully.

Grey and Rosa watching from across the room, track June and Charles as they walk up the stairs, a sight to be seen! Charles, the badass from late in the 20th century adorned in early century formal attire, escorting a lovely redhead half his age; June, the lovely redhead has gained the attention of every man in the room, including a man, slight of build with long black hair, who is watching her ascend the stairs as he walks towards Mata Hari.

Grey watches as he approaches her.

The man, perfectly put together, spends way more time on his looks than Grey ever would. He puts out his hand to Mata Hari when he arrives; rising out of the chair she stands and looks at the floor while he talks to her about something. The man seems to be scolding her.

Suddenly something clicks in Grey's brain! Both Mata Hari and this stranger have a similar build, body structure and stance, even the hair is similar. They could be brother and sister; they must have similar heritage.

Grey wonders.

Watching from the small cafe adjacent to the lobby, and knowing that all is well, Grey stops looking at them too look at his table-mate Rosa, and says, "I'd say all is good. Let's eat."

"Deal, I'm starving Marvin" she replies, smiling.

Grey notices how beautiful she is when she smiles. All the lines created by the trials and tribulations of her life, of war and stress, and now the tripper life, leaves her face. She looks 20 years younger. In fact she seems to look younger and younger each year; maybe this tripper lifestyle is as good for her as it is for him.

"May I say again, how lovely you look today." Grey says.

"No, you may not." She coils her right hand into a fist and prepares to punch him as she naturally would. Feeling a collective pause in the small cafe, she quickly drops her arm and resumes her prim and proper behavior, much to Grey's pleasure.

"Now mi-lady, what would you like to eat today? Some tea and crumpets perhaps?" he asks.

Grey winces as she toe kicks him under the table.

"Yes, that would be lovely my dear, and then perhaps some real food, huh. Something more fitting of a warrior. Something I can sink my teeth into and actually taste, how about some animal protein?" She says.

"Wonderful." Grey raises his hand to gain the attention of the attendant, he looks at Rosa with extreme eye contact, "Sounds delightful." She has no choice but to laugh.

CHAPTER SEVENTEEN

Miokel enters the French Armenian Legion office through the simple front door. To call it an office would be an overstatement. The room contains one large wooden table with six dilapidated chairs, a few bullet holes that decorate the stucco walls, and a skinny hallway that goes out the back, probably to a holding cell. There are three legionaries squatting off to one side throwing dice into the corner and one doing paperwork at the table. Miokel approaches the one working at the table.

"Afternoon sir." He says.

The man keeps working.

Miokel spots the insignia on his uniform, the three chevrons on his shoulder marking him as a Staff Sergeant, and decides to address him accordingly, "Good afternoon Chef." He says.

The man stops working and leans back in his chair to look up at Miokel. He sees a man of Persian descent standing before him, not dressed as they normally would be, but as one who is a traveler, an adventurer. Dirt and dust cover his clothing, yet he is cleaner than his clothes. I wonder what he wants....

"Is your officer around Chef?" Miokel asks.

The man finally speaks.

"We have none." The staff sergeant replies, "He was killed a few days ago. I am filling out the paperwork now."

"Times are tough, huh." Miokel says.

The legionnaire smiles, "Yes, yes they are."

Miokel knows from history, there are about 1,000 men in the French Armenian Legion. He also knows most of them die in the coming battles. Based on historical statistics, of the four legionnaires in the room, only one will survive the war.

Miokel grabs the back of a chair, "May I sit? I have something of interest and since you are the senior man, it would be you I should talk to about it."

The man nods in approval and says, "Who are the two on the porch?"

Miokel replies as he gains his chair, "Two Advisors from America. They are, how shall we say, getting a finger on the pulse of what is going on around here. They only speak English and one is female, so I left them on the porch."

The Staff sergeant looks over at the three playing dice, "Good move."

The man looks Miokel up and down. Chef Agnuni has pretty good instincts, hell he is still alive after years of the French Armenian Legion, and years of this life has perfected his instinct and ability to read people. It seems most the people he and the legionnaires encounter, try to lie to them in one way or another. This man he is not so sure about yet. He wants to like him instinctually but there is something different about him. Either way, it is part of his job to keep the peace in this area and that sometimes looks like listening to the locals and their troubles. They do occasionally bring some valid issues to the table.

"What is it I can help you with sir?" the Chef asks.

"Not sir." Miokel puts out his hand, "Miokel if you would."

The man takes his offered hand in a handshake, "Miokel it is."

He drops his hand to his empty tea cup. Disappointed in its emptiness he gathers himself up to get another, "Would you like some tea?" he asks Miokel.

"I would, thank you." He replies.

The man gets up and ambles toward the skinny hallway, his stockiness apparent when his shoulders rub one wall or the other as he disappears down it. Miokel hears a door open and close.

Glancing over his shoulder and out the still open front door, Miokel cannot see Mac and John, but he can hear them chatting quietly to each other. They are on the steps watching the culture walk by them. The ultimate beauty of this job to Miokel is getting to witness on every trip, the many ways of life and cultures he reads about in history. He has learned that many, many times the way it is presented in historical documentation is not what it was really like.

Hearing the door down the hall open again, he turns his attention back into the room. The three in the corner have stopped their play and are watching him. He nods to them and asks to play, "Mind if I join in?" their eyes light up with greed. Miokel makes to get up and join them, when their Chef, the most senior man alive, finishes banging his way down the hall and into the room. He shakes his head at Miokel, "Before you know it, they will have all your money, clothes, and you will have signed over to them as slaves, the Americans you are keeping outside for their safety."

Miokel laughs a good hearty laugh. Looking at the men in the corner he settles back into his chair while smiling at them, "Maybe later," He says to them directly, "Business first."

They scowl, knowing that he brings bad news and something to do.

"My name is Agnuni by the way Miokel." He says as he sits back into his chair, "Agnuni Zinvorian." He looks at both cups for a minute and then sets one in front of Miokel, having determined which one he had been drinking out of before. Completely tea stained, it was an obvious choice.

Miokel takes the cup and raises it, "Thank you Agnuni, son of a soldier. It seems this is not a new profession for your family, you come by it honestly."

"Thank you Miokel. Come by it honestly, what does that mean?" Agnuni asks.

Miokel is surprised. Damn! Where did he pick that up? It must be from spending time with June and her southern speaking language mix. She must've said it and he picked it up in its proper context without knowing it.

"It means you get it from your family, in this case from your father and probably his father before. It is a family trait." Miokel answers.

Agnuni nods, "True, so true. I am from generations of fighters." he looks at Miokel.

Miokel takes a sip of his tea, it is hot and spicy. It is great stuff! Putting it down, he nods his liking to Agnuni. He also ignores the look, knowing he is being sized up.

"And you, you are from a long line of explorers or something like that aren't you? Traders or mercenaries, I can't decide which." Agnuni says.

Miokel, stoic as per normal says, "A little of both."

They chat and finish their tea, similar in their adventurous lineage; it is easy for them to talk. They cover upbringings and the call to adventure, the current war in action, how the Germans are attempting to take over the world, and killings of his brethren.

After a while, the conversation winds down and Miokel decides that enough small talk has occurred, way more than covering the traditional small-talk time, before getting down to asking for favors.

"So I fear I have kept the Americans waiting long enough, I must get down to business." Miokel says.

"Let me get us more tea, then we will commence." Agnuni says. He starts to get up as one of the relentless dice players happens to be walking by. The legionnaire grabs his cup and Miokel's without asking and heads down the hall.

The tea handled, now is as good a time as any.

"We have word that an escaped prisoner is headed this way to partake in some espionage. She will be traveling with a French spy and is in route to trade for jewels. These jewels are intended to be used to help fund France's battles and war efforts in general." Miokel says.

"This sounds like a good thing." Agnuni says.

"It would be," Miokel continues, "It would be if they were going to take them back to France. We have secure word that the intention by the spy is to steal the jewels and kill the woman. We need this woman to go back to France for political reasons. It is important to the cause that she stands trial. The reasons and details are unknown to me. To be honest, I don't care about that part. I care about getting her back on a ship headed to France and..." Miokel pauses. He looks at the man in charge to feel out where he is on what Miokel is pitching to him. No worries so far. "...and kill the spy. He has betrayed France on several occasions and we need to put an end to that. Here, far from his influences, is a great place and time to rid France of him."

"If he is here for jewels, he must be meeting somebody important. Nobody around here can hold on to jewels without the word spreading quickly, and then either the thieves and thugs or Agha Petros and his men will be after them. It is all over then, Agha is a..." the men across the room look up. Agnuni Zinvorian chooses his words carefully, fear enters, well not fear, but caution, caution enters his body as he speaks.

"I, we have a strong belief that he is not whom he seems, and may be responsible for many of our brethren's deaths." He says.

Miokel now knows Agnuni trusts him or he would never have said that.

He is in.

"We believe that as well. Although a man of that position, it is hard to prove. That may be later, if at all. Right now, we have this mission. And some of the end results of this mission will hurt Agha Petros directly. More financially, than anything else; maybe politically as well, who knows." Miokel says.

"But that is not your mission." Agnuni says.

"Correct." Miokel replies, "My mission is to make sure the jewels and the escaped prisoner get into the hands of mother France and to make sure the spy gets dead."

Agnuni looks at him, "How can I help with this, this mission of yours? I have only four of us left. Who knows when replacements will arrive, if at all. I have nothing to offer."

"Actually, you do." Miokel says.

"What do I have to offer?" Agnuni asks.

"You are the French Legion outpost here; you have all the power of France. The spy will bring her here while figuring things out locally. You will then know what they both look like. It will be a great help."

"Why don't we just grab them then?" Agnuni asks before answering his own question, "Because we need to locate the jewels."

Miokel nods, "Because of the jewels."

Both men sit there, letting the last words hang in the room. Miokel sips his second cup of tea. Since Agnuni Zinvorian is an NCO and the highest ranking man left, it is up him to make the decision.

All is quiet as he thinks, a few flies buzz around the room. Mackenzie and John chat quietly on the porch, providing a surreal background noise.

The sounds of dice rolling have stopped, his men awaiting Agnuni's response. Miokel, sipping his tea, is the loudest sound in the room.

"Ok, but first I must contact France. I know I cannot ask about the spy but I can confirm this woman's escape. When they confirm, then we will help." He says.

Miokel smiles, he likes this guy. He appreciates that he wants to confirm the story; it says good things about him. He will be a good ally for sure.

Both men stand up and shake hands. Chef Zinvorian

walks Miokel to the front door in order to grab a glance at the Americans outside if nothing else. "The telegraph is down the street. I will find you where afterwards?" he asks Miokel.

"You will find us at the only hotel in town." Miokel responds, "We will be checking in there."

Miokel walks outside. Mackenzie and John get up; they have indeed been sitting on the steps and passing the time. All walk off without a word.

Barking orders to his troops, Agnuni watches the three walk off. They are talking in English, not a language he understands, maybe someday.

Turning around, he sees the one legionnaire holding his Chef's cover and weapon for him. He takes them, puts on his cover, and straps on the leather war belt holding his revolver.

"This will be interesting, interesting indeed, no matter what the telegram response is." Agnuni says to no one in particular.

CHAPTER EIGHTEEN

The next day, Grey and Rosa head outside, setting the gears in motion on their breakout mission.

Walking into the street, with nary a word, they arrive in the middle of it. Streams of manual laborers walk up and down the streets, forming long lines and leading from the port, towards the destination of the cargo they carry on their heads and shoulders. It would seem this port located in the eastern area of the Mediterranean Sea is thriving in this time of war. It's hard to tell what the goods being hauled are, as they either head from the port or to the port, wrapped in burlap or contained in baskets. Many of the burlap sacks and baskets contain food and basic materials, whilst others are sure to contain guns, ammo and other tools of war. Either would be lucrative to smuggle.

The owner of said goods is sure to be the one running the area. This port town and the surrounding area for miles, in any direction, are controlled by someone. Usually just one someone, with a private army of some kind; sometimes they are a military leader stationed in the area running their own smuggling operations and other times it is a local, yet still a private enterprise.

According to provided history, these goods Grey and Rosa are watching walk to and fro, aren't here and this isn't happening. There is nothing in written history to tell them who to look for, and where to find them. They will have to use different methods.

Rosa turns to Grey, "Well, where do we start? We have nothing to go on. Other than the jewels we are looking for are in this town, or will be here very soon. How do we find them?"

Grey stands there watching all the laborers walking to and fro with their loads of goods, "I would say whoever is in charge of all this illegal trade is a good place to start."

"Great, where do we find him?" Rosa says.

Grey turns his head and points, "I would say. . .there."

Rosa looks. He is pointing to a house on top of a hill, the tallest hill around. From its walls and roof, one would be able to see far into the Mediterranean Sea, and able to see all that goes on in the town below. That will be the spot they would set up residence. It's the spot either her or Grey would pick, or anybody else for that matter.

Without another word, they turn and start walking the streets and pathways, meandering and finding their way into good locations to scope out the building on the hill, they work their way through the town's streets. Seeking vantage point after vantage point, they reconnoiter the house on the hill as they approach. By the time they get near it, Grey has a plan.

He lays it out for Rosa, "It would seem there are no guards, or if there are, they are well hidden and none are on patrol. Perhaps this guy has the area so well controlled that he doesn't even need an army of his own."

"Or perhaps they are out controlling the worker bees." Rosa says, pointing behind them at all the activity.

"Perhaps, but here's what I am going to go with, he has no reason for it. All these people are on his side. Perhaps it's because he is giving them a way to live without fighting, or maybe he is from this village and he has created so much fear that he no longer needs to guard his house." Grey says.

"Hmm." is all Rosa says in reply.

"My alarms are not going off, so I'd say if we sneak up there, we may just find what we are looking for." Grey says.

"Ok. You're gunny; I'm good with the plan." She says.

Grey long ago got used to her nickname for him, even though he never officially served in any military.

They work their way up the hillside, through an orchard of trees. Out of season, the trees sit dormant and wait. Under the surface, their roots grow and strengthen, while the buds on the branches prepare to blossom. The leaves lay broken and crispy on the ground from a six-month beating.

The future fruit pickers and tree pruners are carrying smuggled goods around in the town below, leaving the orchard devoid of activity.

At the edge of the orchard, they settle in for a last look-see of the house on the hill. A few servants walk about, focused on their tasks with intention. No men or guards are in the line of site. In fact, it is so low key that Grey wonders if his instincts are wrong, and this is not the location of the local leader. Then faintly, from an upstairs window, he hears some sounds of passion: a few faint moans, a quiet conversation and several female giggles.

Apparently he does live here and is occupied. Perfect.

"This is the place." Grey says.

"Why, because he is having sex during the day? Don't you ever have sex during the day?" Rosa says.

Grey grimaces, "Of course I do. . .just not with several at once." Those female giggles filter down from the upstairs window again.

"Ok, ok." Rosa says, grinning.

The two find their way across a small clearing and inside the house, through a door-less opening on their side of the house. Pausing to let their eyes adjust to the dim light inside, they see they are on the edge of an outdoor hallway, with doors off to either side. The hall is open to the environment, a perfect breeze graces Grey and Rosa as they step into it.

Off to one side, about a meter or so from where they stand adjusting their eyes, is a stairway going up and into the wall to the right. A few quiet scuffs are heard coming down the stairs; they flatten against the walls, instantly deciding to wait it out. A small woman walks down the stairs and turns to walk into the breeze and away from them. The servant woman is smiling and shaking her head.

Grey and Rosa detach from the wall's shadows and take the stairs. Quick and quiet they make their way to the top floor of the big house. Coming to the top, they find themselves in another breezeway, with doors off each side and at the far end, it makes a turn to the right. The two stand at the top of the stairs and at the end of the hall.

Quietly they walk down the hall, owning it instead of slinking down it. Stopping and listening at each of the doors before opening them. They find nothing exciting behind the first couple of doors. Putting ears to the third door on the left, it has them listening to the frolicking going on inside. They avoid this door for now. If they don't find what they are looking for elsewhere they will have to enter it and make decisions from there.

After listening, Grey and Rosa open the door across the hall from the afternoon sojourn. Finding an office, they realize they might not get to join in on the fun after all. Inside is a big desk full of clutter, a few chairs loosely gathered around a table with half-consumed bottles of liquor in the center and a few ungracefully aging maps, not much else of note.

Walking around the backside of the desk, Grey does find something. A small, salty air rusted safe sits on the floor and a few more bottles of alcohol sit on top. As well as a couple of used glasses, the door to the safe is closed.

Rosa walks up, "Well I can blow that lock off in a heartbeat. Of course, the love parade across the hall will surely hear it. So we may have to handle them also."

"No." Grey says, "This is a quiet mission. We are not looking to blow stuff up and leave evidence, this time, my dear. Sorry."

Rosa looks disappointed.

"Well maybe this guy is so confident, he doesn't even lock it." She says as she reaches down. She runs her fingers around the edges of the door, checking for clips, wires or pressure release devices, she finds none. Without asking she grabs the safe's handle and twists it. The safe clicks.

She looks up at Grey. Seriously!

Rosa gently pulls on the safe door, it resists at first until the vacuum is broken, then it opens with ease. The lack of squeak in the hinges tells us that, in spite of the exterior rust, the safe door is opened frequently. Somebody is doing well.

Several sacks are contained within the floor safe. Rosa reaches in and grabs them both. Handing them to Grey she stands up, pushing the safe door mostly closed with her toe. He loosens the strings holding one of the sacks closed and pulls the material gathered at the top apart. Lifting it closer to his face, he looks down inside. The smell of dust and dirt enters his nostrils. As does an indecipherable smell, perhaps rocks?

He reaches in and pulls one of the rocks out. Both his and Rosa's eyes go wide. Jackpot! In his hand is a rough-cut jewel, rough and glasslike, it could be a diamond. He reaches in again and finds more of the same. One more time he reaches in and this time, he brings up a rock with more of a reddish hue to it.

Rosa grabs the other bag and opens it. Inside she finds gems of green and blue. Looking up at Grey she grins ear to ear. She mouths at him, "Jackpot! Let's get out of here." No sound escaping her lips.

He pulls the strings closed on the bag he is holding and puts it deep in the hidden pockets of his suit. Putting his hand out, he requests the other from Rosa. She pulls the strings closed and puts it deep in the same pocket of his, somehow finding it through the suits illusion.

Both find their way back to the door and after listening, open it and take the center of the hallway once more.

Moans and groans can be heard from the door across from them. Words of encouragement from a few female voices, and the moans of pleasure from another mix with the primal grunts of a man.

Grey and Rosa shake their heads as they make their way down the back stairs again. Pausing at the bottom, they see the coast is clear. Making their way out the back and into the orchard, which once again is uneventful.

Shortly, they are back on the edge of town and working its pathways back towards their base of operations. There is a spring in their step; never in their wildest dreams did they think this part of the mission would be that easy. Both had visions of gunfights, explosions and cannon fire when contemplating this part of the mission.

"Man, I feel like I am playing that game my brother talked me into playing twice as a kid. I thought it was lame, but he and his friends would play it for an entire day. They just called it D&D. I called it lame." Rosa says.

"Ok." Grey says.

Rosa laughs, "What I am saying is, we would go on these adventures with these characters they created and come to these rooms where the jewels were just laying around. After entering a room, the geek in charge of the game would roll some dice and would say 'You find 10 jewels, or 2 Elven swords or...' The point is, they were just laying around, unprotected and unlocked. I never thought I would find that in real life."

Grey himself has to smile, it does seem too easy, but then again, who says everything in life has to be hard.

"Let's not take any chances, though." he says.

"Agreed." Rosa says, "Let's get out of here."

They head back into town. The few miles of walking gives them some exercise, other than that, their heart rates don't even rise. Such is how easy it was.

Who says it has to be hard, and what do they know....

*****

Two figures walk the dirt street. There is a spring to their step as they weave their way through the throngs of laborers working their long meandering lines from one destination to another.

The two figures are unencumbered. He is an imposing figure, with a long gray beard, she a smaller statuesque Spanish woman who wears her dress perfectly.

As they walk one notices they must be adventurers, she with her leather boots sneaking out from under her dress, and he with his weathered face, both with their confident walk. There is an air of confidence that comes with an adventurer.

A port town such as this is used to sailors, adventurers and other types of travelers, yet there is something different about these two. A hero-walk of sorts, like they know they are doing something for the greater good.

CHAPTER NINETEEN

June is prepping in her room. Excited about this part of the mission, she gets to dress up and go to a ball!

She lays out her corset and dress onto the bed, gathers up her stockings and shoes and places them on the bed as well. It seems the tripper suit will not hold up to the critical eyes of the upper echelon in this area, so she gets to wear real clothes, even better!

June is just about to pull her off her tripper suit when she hears boots gathering outside her door. She pauses, hand on the release.

The door bursts open, and several men breach the threshold. She tries screaming as they enter, but one is quick enough to jump on the bed and grab her from behind. He slaps a hand over her face, the pain stops her voice before it exits.

The three men all do their part to restrain her; one holding her face and head from behind, the other two grabbing a leg and a wrist each.

June is unable to move, her legs and arms held out and down, her face turned up slightly and head back. She faces the wall and window, her back to the door and her butt on the bed.

Smells of last night's alcohol, old pee, and sweat enter her nostrils. It is oozing off the men around her, putrefying the air.

Her eyes wide, she watches the two men in front of her as they hold her in submission. They have evil in their eyes but not rape. She relaxes a bit. Well, not really.

She hears boot steps entering the room. What sounds like a man, works his way around the bed and steps in front of her.

The steps did indeed belong to a man. She doesn't know it yet, but Lee Batard stands before her, a representative of France. He intends to know why she is here.

"Why are you here?" he asks her.

June looks at him wide eyed.

"Why are you here?" he asks her again.

June narrows he eyes at him.

"You are here to bugger with my plans aren't you! I have been informed of this!" He leans in and pinches the cartilage of her nose between two of his fingers. He squeezes to cause pain but not break it, not yet at least.

June is wondering who he is and who would have told him about her. She knows it would be none of her team, and is doubtful Mata Hari would have. The woman obviously despises her capturer. Wait, this must be him, her capturer! Who talked...?

"You are not going to talk so easy. I can tell." He addresses his men, "Let's take her somewhere I can talk to her without worrying about noise, and I am sure her protector will come back up the front stairs any moment now. We are lucky he walked away." Lee Batard directs this last statement at June.

The men stand up and carry her over the bed, out of the room and into the hall. Hurrying for the back staircase, used only by the help, they whisk her away.

Lee Batard takes a quick glance around the room, seeing nothing he wants to quickly grab, he walks out of the room and down the same staircase his cronies took June down. As he exits the hotel into an alley, he thinks about a strange encounter on the street when he and Mata Hari first arrived in town.

He was walking the street with purpose with the next several days of plans in his head. Lost in thought, he is paying little attention to what is going on around him. He is rapidly approaching a man leaning against a building, at the end of an alleyway. The man appears to be waiting for something.

Finally, Lee Batard senses his presence. Breaking his concentration, he looks up and sees a strangely dressed man. The man has goggles around his neck, leather gauntlets on his arms and a strange sleeveless leather trench coat; he is wearing it over a stereotypical stripped shirt. The man seems to have an affiliation with motor gears, he has a few placed on his leather gauntlets and his hatband.

As Lee approaches, the man stands up straight and readies himself.

Lee Batard gets ready to fight. He keeps walking, though.

"No need for that." The strange man says.

"Then why are you readying yourself?" Lee Batard says.

"Because I am waiting for you fine sir." The stranger says.

The man is smiling at Lee Batard.

"How is it you would know I am coming through here?" Lee Batard asks.

He is still ready to fight, the stranger hasn't relaxed yet either.

"Life is strange Mr. Batard, very strange indeed, more than you will ever know." the stranger says, "It would take me longer to explain it all than we have time to talk, I am afraid. Regardless, I will tell you I know about your plans with Mata Hari and Agha Petros, not to mention the big bag of jewels you will be taking back to France with you."

The stranger has Lee Batard's attention; nobody outside his head knows his plans. He has spoken them to no one, well except for his prisoner that is, and she is bound and guarded on the steamer still. He just walked away from the steamer moments ago.

Lee Batard examines the man's face a little more. He has straight dark brown hair, distinguished eyebrows, and a sneaky mischievous look about him. The look on the strangers' face currently says, "I am waiting for this man to decide what to do."

Lee Batard makes his decision and having decided what weapon to pull, reaches for it. He at all times carries a two-shot derringer and a needle dagger. For this stranger, he is going straight for the derringer.

"I wouldn't." The stranger says.

Lee Batard looks at him. The stranger is standing even on both feet, no attempts to reach for a weapon have been made, yet the look on his face has switched from indifference to pity. Like he knows Lee Batard will die, has no doubt in fact. Yet he stands there, still and motionless.

Confused, Lee Batard hesitates, "Why don't you just say your piece and we will part ways, never to see each other again. If we do, I'm killing you on sight." He says.

"Deal." the stranger replies.

"There is someone who is going to mess with your plans. A few someones actually; they work as a team of seven, sometimes dividing and conquering their resources to get things done. I don't know exactly their plans as I do yours. It hasn't happened yet.

However, I do know they arrived today, just as you did. Well not in the same way, but you know. Got to town today." the stranger says.

This guy is a little on the lunatic side, Lee Batard thinks as he continues to listen. The stranger quickly gives him identifying features on all seven people and a general idea of what they might try.

Even if this guy is a lunatic, Lee Batard is glad for the reminder to be cautious. He is a spy for France, off of her protective shores, and in an area of the world in total flux. Even Agha Petros, his friend, informed him to be careful here, it is about to get worse than it already is.

Lee Batard stands there in his same at the ready stance, as the stranger finishes what he has to say.

The stranger apparently has said everything he came here to say. As soon as he stops talking, he tips his hat and smiles. While placing his hat, gears and all back on his head, he turns and walks down the alley.

With the stranger's back turned to Lee Batard's, he can now shoot him if he wants. Not afraid to shoot anyone in the back, the thought does cross his mind. Yet, he lets it go. His instincts tell him the man is trying to help, what concerns Lee is he does not know why.

Lee Batard resumes his previous course, heading for his friend Agha Petros. With all of his spy senses on alert, he focuses again on his plan, although it is harder to do than it was a moment ago.

He keeps thinking about that stranger knowing his plans. How is it possible? Perhaps everything is not as it seems. He will have to pay extra attention. Maybe Agha Petros is going to attempt a double cross, take the girl and keep the diamonds. Lee Batard knows it is not beneath him to do something like that, Agha has flexible morals, after all, usually flexing in the direction of his biggest advantage.

CHAPTER TWENTY

Charles walks up the stairs, his prize in his hand. June deserves a flower for her gown, and he has found some great specimens for her to try out. He knows she will be ecstatic!

Walking up the stairs with purpose, he focuses on the flowers, making sure they are not jostled or injured during the journey. They were hard to come by, and he wants them to be pristine when she sees them. He knows they will make her day.

Reaching the top of the stairs, Charles sees the third door on the left open. Damn! What is she up too?

Hurrying just a bit, while still being cautious with the flowers, he gets to the door quickly. Entering, he sees the room is empty, her gown and the rest of her formal attire on the bed. Charles smells fear, cheap alcohol and old sweat, intermingled with June's perfume.

DAMN, something has happened to her!

He drops the flowers to the floor. The petals explode on impact, flinging in all directions. Their savory scents intermingle with the smell of fear.

Charles runs out the door and towards the back stairs,

determined to track whoever grabbed June and recover his team member he is sworn to protect team member.

This is worse than "not good," he thinks as he runs down the stairs. Reaching bottom, he heads for a nearby exit and rapidly leaves the building. Looking in both directions, he sees one end of the alley is a dead end while the other heads for the street.

Running, he heads for the street. Bursting out the end of the alley and into the main street, he skids to a stop, creating a cloud of dust. Looking up and down the road, he sees nothing but humans with loads of goods on their heads. There is no one with curly red hair.

*****

Grey and Rosa saunter down the street, not in a hurry, nothing to do until the formal ball later, they take in the local surroundings.

"Can't wait to see you all dressed up in 1900's regalia!" Rosa says.

"Whatever!" Grey responds, blushing.

"Haha! That is awesome! I made you blush!" Rosa chortles.

"You did indeed. You caught me off guard. I'm still in super-serious mission mode," he says.

"When aren't you in super-serious mission mode?" she asks.

"Good point." Grey says, "There is history to that."

He is walking slower than usual, spending that extra view time to take in the locals, observe their architecture, smell their foods, and appreciate their women as they walk by. Not one to allow himself sex while on a mission, there are times he longs to connect with the women he runs into during his missions. When else would he be able to meet women of this time and culture? This is why he lives inside his virtual vacation system because there he allows the fantasy and connection.

His eye goes to a particularly voluptuous woman ahead of them on the street. He can't help but sneak a good peek, and he is well into it when his peripheral vision picks out a commotion off in the distance, at the edge of his vision.

Instantly his eyes refocus on the movement in the distance.

He sees a woman being carried by three men; she is putting up a fight, kicking and screaming as they carry her from an alley next to a hotel, across the street and to another alley on the other side. The woman is yelling her redhead off and calling them names. She manages to get a leg free and kicks one of them in the head. He quickly regains his purchase on her leg, acting like nothing ever happened. He sneaks a blow to her midsection as punishment regardless.

Wait! Redhead and hotel--the only ones in the town of each!

Rosa speaks first, "Grey!"

"I see it!" he says.

"You keep tabs on them, I'll go check on Charles, and then we'll catch up. Go!" Grey says as he takes off running also but he slows his run to Rosa's pace--not wanting to lose her in the throngs. After all, there might be other bad guys about. Weaving her way between people burdened with heavy loads, Rosa picks her way through, quickly and efficiently. Within seconds, she and Grey split ways.

*****

Charles stands in the middle of the main street despising himself and his choice to leave the hotel to get flowers. Then he spots Rosa running in his direction. Charles looks behind her and then takes one more look behind him. He sees nothing to indicate June or a scuffle of any kind.

Rosa gets close enough to communicate and she points into an alleyway directly across from the one Charles just burst out of. Charles looks down the alley as Rosa runs by him. Seeing nothing, he trusts her and follows her; she must've seen something somehow, a miracle of miracles.

They run through the alley, seeing nothing but remnants of a cluster of boot prints. Fresh ones. Knowing the boot prints contain the answer to who has June, they follow them quickly.

*****

Lee Batard and his goons had no problems getting June to their home base. No one batted an eye as they carried her from alley to alley and into the flophouse. Once in the flophouse, hungry eyes and desire was all that they saw in the eyes of those who happened to notice their prize. One even asked if they could have her when they were done. Lee Batard considered this as they took her up a flight of stairs and into the first door on the right.

This room has a strange history; it has been used as a

manager's office, a doctor's office and a viewing room. Entering the door off of the hallway put them into the main room, off the back side of this room is another door and to the left of it is a strange thing, a window. When it was a viewing room, customers would pay by the minute to watch unmentionable things occurring on the other side of the glass. One's imagination is the only limit to what could've been paid for in this ancient port town.

Accompanied by his three goons, Lee Batard took June through the entry room and into the back room. Confident that June is secure here, Lee decided that he only needed one of his cronies to assist in June's interrogation to see if they can extract any information from this mysterious redhead.

In order to speed up the process of locating Agha Petros, Lee dispatches his other two goons to find Agha's location.

"You two go and find Agha Petros. I need to talk to him!" Lee Batard barks.

"Can we get paid first?" one of the goons inquires.

"Like you would come back if I did?" Lee Batard responds.

"Well, we don't trust you!" the other one says.

"Yah! You need to at least pay us half first!" The first one is quite livid by now.

Disgusted and not wanting to waste time arguing with idiots, Lee Batard opts to pay them half. Knowing there is a chance they will just settle for the lesser sum and not come back. For the sake of time, he takes the gamble. If they run on him, he will find them later and kill them.

He gives the two goons half of the monies coming to them, and they take off.

They exit the room and head the opposite way they came in. Entering a room at the very end of the hall, they visit their source, wanting to get their opium head on before wandering the streets looking for Agha Petros. He could be anywhere this time of the day. He likes to ride the early evening streets in his new automobile and randomly disperse money and praise, while selectively delving out punishment and death to those deemed worthy of it. This strange combination seems to keep the smugglers loyal and happy; it's the right mix of love and strict, brutal justice.

*****

Grey takes the steps into the hotel three at a time. He bursts into the lobby, instantly feeling a fool. All is normal and everyday occurrence until he runs in. They all freeze to watch him realize what an idiot he looks like to them. Tipping a mock hat, he makes his way over to the main stairs, trying to make himself look nonchalant and failing miserably. After a few steps, he abandons the effort and takes the stairs at the double time.

Reaching the top, Grey runs into the open doorway of June's room, seeing signs of a struggle and flowers on the floor, but no blood or Charles, he exits and hurries towards the back stairs. Grey has taken the back stairs a few times, as much to switch up his routine and check them out and where they go, he knows they will lead to the alley June and her captures emerged from.

He descends the stairs two at a time, steep and windy; this is all he can manage. Within seconds Grey is at the backdoor, he quickly pushes himself through and into the alley. His attention is to the alley across the way; he sees Rosa and Charles disappearing into the distance.

Good news! Now let's see if I can catch up!

*****

Following the cluster of footprints, Charles and Rosa exit onto another roadway. They look up and down it as they continue on through to the alley on the other side. Rosa and Charles, now running together as fast as possible, try to catch up to their teammate and her capturers.

They both stop in their tracks! Looking at each other, they realize the cluster of boot prints they were tracking have disappeared. Turning around, they slowly scope the limestone dust until they see where the footprints tromped off to.

They scope the ground's details, backtracking about 1/3 of the way down the alley until they reach a doorway. Looking up, they see an old dilapidated sign swinging aimlessly above the door. Neither of them can read it, but the currency list alongside each of the four lines of writing tells them it is probably a low-end flop house. With its entrance off of an alley, it sets the necessary tone.

Rosa and Charles make eye contact. Their eyes ask each other, "Are you ready?" and respond with a resounding, "You know I am!"

Rosa reaches for the door; she notices several bullet holes and other signs of reckless wear and tear. She pulls it open for Charles to enter first, and takes note of his game face. She knows he will kick in every door, and take on the entire population of this flophouse if that's what it takes to find June. She enters behind him, her face showing the same grit.

CHAPTER TWENTY-ONE

John spent as much time as possible sitting out on the balcony, most of this day in fact.

The balcony is located on the third floor of the hotel; it keeps him out of the dust moving about on the street below. Occasionally some horses go racing by or that damn car does, causing a billowing of cream dust, which does its best to settle over each and all. It is indiscriminate.

He has mostly had the balcony to himself. Although the balcony is shared by the occupants of the room next door, the next door neighbor has kept to himself.

John knows people are into some strange things, he has tried some strange things in his life, but this guy is at a different level. Instead of hanging out on the balcony, like John was hoping he would do, this man has been inflicting self-punishment of some kind and with a strap or belt from the sounds of it. John is not sure what it is all about, but his neighbor spends a lot of time crying and wailing, seeking penitence from the devil himself. Apparently he has let him down on several occasions and will use the war to make up for it.

At the moment, though, all is quiet next door. John can

hear the man walking about his room on occasion, recently the sound of a drawer opening, that's about it. It has been quiet there for awhile, the punishment is over for the day or the moment at least. Getting close to time for the ball, he is probably getting ready, whatever that looks like for him.

Based on what Miokel told him about this man and what he has witnessed today, John is glad they are handling this bastard of a man, he is a weird cuss and has issues. If what Lee Batard does to himself is any indication, John is pretty sure this thing with Mata Hari is not the first of its kind and it would not be the last. The team's plan is becoming more and more likable, each time John thinks of it.

It is quiet in John's room also. Miokel and Mackenzie are not in at the moment. Miokel and Grey decided it is best to grab Lee Batard before the ball, keeping him out of the way for when June approaches Mata Hari. Grey and Rosa are seeking out the jewels at the moment as well. Their goal is to obtain the jewels undetected from whomever in this town has them; Grey said something about heading to the house on the hill and taking it from there, whatever that means. All John knows is he is left holding down the fort while the rest of the team is out gallivanting. Except for Charles and June that is, they have kept an intentional distance from the rest of the tripper team, as part of their cover. John is sure they are getting ready for the ball.

John has enjoyed the downtime his assigned task has provided; it gave him an opportunity to think about the night before this latest mission's tram ride. Grey did not lead him astray. Man, she was awesome! She was a great way to spend an evening, and money well spent. He is glad Grey is the kind to lead without judgment about his personal life. Rather, the opposite in this case.

Looking out over the balcony, John sees Miokel and Mackenzie fast approaching, Agnuni and his three Armenian legionnaires on their heels.

John smiles, apparently the NCO in charge as decided to help them out, good news!

John cants an ear in the direction of the room next door, not many sounds are escaping, but he can tell there is someone there.

Miokel and crew disappear as they get closer, the balcony blocking them from view. John decides to sit exactly where he is as he waits for them to come up the room.

After just a few minutes they arrive, entering the room without knocking or speaking, all seven of them now occupy a room big enough for about three of them.

Miokel mouths to John, "Is he there?" while pointing next door. John nods his head. Miokel looks at Agnuni and nods his head; silently they put a plan in motion.

Two of the legionnaires walk back out the door into the hall while Agnuni and the other head out onto the balcony. It seems they will either wait here, just in case or enter Lee Batard's room from this side. John hears the door from the hall burst open and some instant shouts. Agnuni and his second walk calmly towards the door to the room off the balcony, a scuffle is still ensuing inside the room.

A loud yelp escapes onto the balcony and loud boot steps head their way. Everyone on the balcony braces themselves. The door to Lee Batard's room bursts open and a man flings himself out of it towards the balcony rail.

Caught off guard, Agnuni reaches for him as he heads for it. He did not expect Lee Batard to take a leap. Based on the telegram he received from France, this was a never die or quit type of man. Suicide didn't fit the telegram.

The man throws himself off the balcony. Three floors above the street, he arches his back in the perfect swan dive. His chest out, arms arched out behind him and his forehead tipped towards the sky.

John watches the man's actions from his assigned post, the chair he has been occupying all day. He sees the look in the man's eyes, crazed and drug filled, his glassy eyes seem joyful and happy. Who knows what is going on in his head? John does wish he knew what he was thinking as he flung himself off the balcony in a perfect swan dive with a grin on his face. One thing John does know, though, this is not Lee Batard. Rather some opium filled lowlife that has found his version of the perfect end to his existence.

They have been bamboozled; Lee Batard has escaped their watch somehow. Miokel looks at John, disappointment on his face.

"I have been here all day!" John says.

"I know." Miokel says, "He outsmarted us, somehow." Miokel looks at Agnuni, "Did one of your guys talk perhaps?"

Agnuni, shakes his head, "Impossible. Not possible. No."

They both stand there looking over the balcony at the body below. The laborers walk around the body, not stopping, heavy loads on their heads and shoulders. A well-dressed couple makes a wide arc around the body. No other notice is taken....

Miokel and Agnuni look at each other. Where is Lee
Batard and what is he up too?

CHAPTER TWENTY-TWO

Grey sets out in a sprint, his goal to catch Rosa and Charles. As he works his way through the long lines of encumbered locals and he wonders how they got the best of Charles, not the laborers, but the three men with June. A strange thought goes through his head about the flowers. Grey knows Charles well enough to know he doesn't have a thing for June. It could be how the bad guys got in, who knows. Would June open the door for someone because they were delivering flowers? He knows the answer, most would. Most wouldn't have to deal with the fact that they were back in 1917 though, and flower delivery was not a thing of the times, at least not around here.

Running, Grey crosses through the next street and alleyway, trying to catch Rosa and Charles. Just as he exits the far end onto another street a large automobile speeds by and almost takes him out, it nearly runs him over! The contents of the automobile: a driver, a well-dressed man in a type of uniform Grey doesn't recognize and a few enforcers. One of them is riding on the back with a submachine gun in hand. He is the only one that pays

Grey any attention. His laugh is the only acknowledgment that Grey was nearly run over. Unbeknownst to both parties, the car is being driven by the man whose jewels were acquired by him and Rosa a short while ago.

Grey hurries across the street, adding that carload of men to his "come back some day and make them pay" list. Colonel Petzer asks him about retirement, that is the closest Grey has to a retirement plan.

He gets clear of the street chaos in time to see his two teammates enter a door off the next alley. Great! They must've found her. He is covering the ground quickly to get to the door. Another, closer door, bursts open into the alley before he can reach the flophouse. Four drunken sailors burst forth, bringing a putrid odor of stale sweat and cheap alcohol. They are drunk and unstable.

One of them literally falls at Grey's feet. Grey is moving so fast he is unable to stop his forward motion. Grey springs off the ground and jumps over the new roadblock, intending to keep moving. Instead, he crashes into two of the three remaining sailors.

They take offense.

Instead of apologizing, Grey tries to keep going, he needs to get through that door and catch up.

One of the sailors grabs him and pulls him back, mumbling something about hurting his buddy.

"You knocked him down." The sailor says.

"Yeah!" another chimes in.

Grey says, "I gotta..." an upward punch to the bottom of his chin cuts him short, it is on for some reason. He doesn't have time to figure out if this is just drunken stupidity or a trap; he has four drunken sailors to deal with!

Before the one on the ground could get up, the other three start throwing punches at Grey, trying to surround him, one comes around to his left. Grey throws him an elbow, he blocks it. Grey brings his left back to guard, just as the sailor in front of him swings in another uppercut. Uppercut is the wrong word, the sailor is just shorter than Grey, he's just aiming for his chin is all. Lucky for Grey, the alcohol has him off his game a bit.

The fallen sailor that started the whole thing may be Grey's saving grace. He is having problems getting off the ground, keeping the numbers a more even 3-1. Grey settles in and sizes up his opponents. The little guy that is in front and to Grey's right has tunnel vision on Grey's chin. He is a strong little dude, and if he connects, Grey is going to feel it. In the meantime the sailor to Grey's left is trying to get behind him, probably to attempt a hold or to smack him in the back of the neck or something else that benefits them in taking out Grey. Regardless, Grey isn't allowing it; Ambidextrous by nature, he is keeping the sailor in line with his left side and is attempting to land backhand fists and elbows, wanting to put him down before the sailor succeeds in getting behind him.

The third sailor is in it halfheartedly, not a natural fighter, he seems confused as to what to do next. He alternates between starting to help his buddy up and participating in the fight. His indecision is what tilts the fight out of balanced poking at each other stage, and moves it to the next level. Mr. Indecisive manages to help his buddy to all four limbs, now with his friend firmly on his hands and knees, he returns to a fighting position.

Grey, still holding his own, is looking for a change and a window of opportunity or something to gain some ground on these four, well three really. Even the third one is only fighting half the time; he seems confused as to what he should be focusing on. Perhaps it's the alcohol or perhaps his buddy laying on the ground is the best fighter in the group, and he wants to get him involved. Who can explain alcohol induced logic....

The sailor reaches down again to help him up and manages to get him to his hands and knees right behind the most actively fighting sailor, the one that threw the first punch. Grey seizes the opportunity and strikes a kick into the gut of said sailor, flipping him over backwards; the sailor summersaults over his buddy and somehow ends up partly underneath him as he collapses.

The sailor to Grey's left also sees an opportunity and takes it. Lunging forward he drives a shoulder into Grey's side, lifting his remaining leg off the ground mid-kick.

Grey smacks the ground hard.

The fight has reached the next level, the stalemate is over.

*****

Having searched the lobby and the rest of the sparsely occupied first floor to no avail, Charles and Rosa race the steps to the second floor. Another long hallway greets them at the top; it is full of doors located on each side of the hallway.

The door on the right is up first. They force the door open and enter the room, Rosa and Charles find themselves in an entry room of sorts, a couple of tables and chairs are in the room, and not much else except some papers scattered about one of the tables. In the far wall is a big glass window and next to this window is a door. Nothing of interest in this front room, so they quickly find themselves peering through said window. Their attention is grabbed, for through the glass and inside the other room are two goons and one curly redhead. All are pissed off and riled up; it is obvious there had been some tussling going on. Unfortunately, the goons have the advantage.

It is also obvious to Charles that June is about to be punched and hit. One goon is holding her from behind. With the other positioned in front of her, it is only a matter of seconds before she will be hit again or worse. It is possible they are up to something else.

It's then that Charles recognizes the goon in front of her, it is the bastard guy, the one that brought Mata Hari here from France, Lee Batard.

Rosa makes a move towards the door. Knowing she won't get there before the Lee Batard has a chance to have at June a few times; Charles decides to go old school ninja. Has no choice in fact.

Reaching up and under the collar of his tripper suit, he pulls out a long heavy needle. Nothing high tech about this needle, in fact, he made it himself out of a cheap tent stake one day while he was waiting for someone. Two needles he made that day; he produced both from the same aluminum stake cut in half and perfectly sharpened on one end. The hows and whys of that story are for another time.

The goon holding June from behind pulls her arms back, which stretches out the whole front of her body, exposing it for Lee Batard to have his way with. He looks her up and down, hungrily, as he picks the targets of his affection. Settling on a few, he first applies a right hook to her gut. The blow causes June to scream in pain. Lee Batard is a strong and accurate cuss; he knows exactly where to hit her to cause the most pain. Next he applies a left jab to her right boob. It's impossible for half of us to imagine what that feels like, although a kick in the nuts may be an indicator. For June, it was an electrical shock that went quickly and brutally through her body followed by a dull, throbbing ache that was sure to linger for days and wander about her body. Unfortunately for June, this was just a light distraction punch applied, in case June was of the tough and trained variety. Its purpose was to give Lee Batard time to reload his right arm. Her face is his next intended target. He wants to break her bones so bad, he is jonesing to do so. The power surges into the muscles and the electrical pulses charge the quick reactors, preparing to release strength forward from the sinewy muscles and into June's jaw with all the intention of shattering it. This bitch must pay!

Pulling the needle free with his left hand while simultaneously taking a step forward with his left, Charles unconsciously lines up the shot in his head. He has done this so many times in practice, the muscle memory is firm and intact. Although he has never had a chance to do it in a real life situation, he knows he will succeed.

Don't take that as these are virgin needles, no! Not true. These needles have pierced the skin of many a man and a few women indeed. They have been thrown and deftly applied by hand on many occasion. The new part, the part he has only done in practice, is the fun part.

The muscles already knowing their job, force his arm to

snap forward as he steps again. Releasing from his earlobe, his wrist snaps stretching the tendons holding it in place; the needle gently held between his thumb and forefinger, races from his hand towards the glass, yes towards the glass. To the needle and the intention behind it, the 1/4 inch thick glass window has the consistency of cheap plastic wrap. It doesn't really exist, even though you are looking at it, it's tangible and yet dissolves at the touch. The needle breezes through with an amazing force of energy, only a smidgen of its energy needed to pierce this deterrent towards its intended target, not even knowing the glass was supposed to stop it.

Before Rosa's brain can register what she just saw, what the silver flash was, the man she is hastily approaching loses all strength and stands there as if someone had just hit the off switch. His muscles clench tightly onto June as the electrical signals malfunction and cause the body to stiffen. A millisecond later his body registers the complete shutdown and he crumbles to the ground, taking June with him.

Lee Batard's punch, hungrily seeking June's face, purely with the intent of crushing it and possibly driving some teeth out the right side cheek as a bonus, is hell bent and well on its way to accomplishing that task when her head miraculously bends back and away from his perfectly aligned bones and the force behind them. It was to be a perfect blow, and her face would have never been the same. Fortunately for June, someone has her back in the most intense way; and they have arrived.

Rosa arriving right about the time Lee Batard registers his miss, announces her presence by helping him to continue moving the energy he is applying to his right arm. Helping the energy to keep moving further than intended, causes Lee Bastard to lose his center and come forward on his toes, which is all Rosa needs to help him spin through his entire center. Her Jujitsu training would call this a throw. Before he could do anything about it, he is spinning through. His face, a moment ago focused on June, is quickly refocusing on the floor, the far wall, the ceiling and quickly coming around again. Landing on his feet, he takes a few steps back; amazingly he lands on his feet in spite of the throws' forces, obviously, he has done so before. Still caught off guard a bit, his less than perfect landing caused some back steps, creating some space between him and Rosa.

She readies herself, she LOVES this part.

Seeing this, Lee Batard grins and loosens up his neck and shoulders, readying himself for some fun.

Rosa and Lee Batard lose no time sizing each other up; rather they actively throw strikes at each other. He comes at Rosa with his pugilist training, years of street fighting and bastardry. She comes at him with Marine martial arts and jujitsu training.

Both close in and throw quick test punches, easily blocked by the other, followed by a few strikes that connect. In a matter of a few seconds, both have landed a few blows.

Undeterred Rosa lets him land one more, building his confidence enough to get him to drop his lower body protection. She then flips a quick forward kick at his groin, her toe the only thing to connect, right in its desired location, the taint.

Now the taint ain't a place many people think about or

are aware of. Heck, who would even consider it a target! But Rosa has learned the hard way that the area is sensitive to both men and women. The feeling of a toe strike to an area overloaded with sensors and nerve endings will put pause to all but the most experienced fighters.

It has the same effect to Lee Batard, he gains a look of shock across his face and takes an involuntary step back while bending forward slightly in a reaction to the pain and shock.

What the hell? Lee Batard thinks. Never has he been struck in the area he was just struck in. The feeling is overwhelming; an urge to poop intermingles with the feeling of a thousand doctor's needles entering body through the small space between his sack and his other unmentionable area. His brain pauses for a second and he finds himself taking an involuntary step back as his butt puckers and tries to turn itself inside out.

Before the pain resides he turns it into anger and prepares to move back into range with this Spanish women standing before him. He doesn't know who she is; he does know someone has trained her. Perhaps she is employed by Spain in a similar fashion as he is employed by France. He will get that out of her later, first he will pummel her for a bit.

Before he can move, Charles is upon him. Too many things going on, somehow he had managed to miss Charles' entry into the room, a huge mistake.

Charles hits him with the force of a professional American Football linebacker. You know the kind; no neck, thigh muscles three feet in diameter, all rage and power. The linebacker tackle from the side forces Lee

Batard off his feet and snaps bones. A ferocious amount of pain overwhelms Lee Batard's body, shutting down the pain receptors in his lower half, somewhat allowing him the use of his legs, a moot point as his body and head hit the block wall. The concussion of brain, skull, and wall coming together under such a force knocks him out, those legs still working for some unknown reason.

Charles erupts from his usual detached professionalism and hammers the guy in the face with his fists. First his right a couple times and then he starts to switch back and forth, holding him up with one hand while proves his point with the other.

Rosa takes a moment to check on June, she seems ok. Looking up at the situation in hand, and seeing rage in Charles, she hurries over and applies a forcible forearm to his chest and pushes him back with it. The interruption allows the unconscious Lee Batard to drop, facedown, in a heap on the floor.

"NO!" she shouts at Charles, "We need him!"

Charles turns away from Lee Batard and checks on the man he killed from afar.

Knowing that Charles feels responsible for losing track of his charge, Rosa leaves him be. He stands and watches the deep purple color spread around the head of the guard. This goon is done. He walks over to the unconscious Lee Batard. This is the guy that was with that Mata Hari woman! He is an obviously bad dude, it oozes out of him. Charles hoists him off the ground and onto his shoulder, not happy that he is not allowed to kill him.

*****

Rosa, Charles and June exit the flophouse into the alley. Rosa gets out the door and then stops in her tracks. Charles, package on his shoulder, hesitates for a second watching her. The look on her face encourages him to look around the corner of the doorframe.

Out in the alley, he sees Grey and four sailors sitting hodgepodge on the ground. All but one of the five are rubbing their chins or other sore spots. Some are still panting. The other, a sailor, is knocked out on the ground.

Charles steps out into the alley, making space for June to peek her head around.

Grey looks up at them, a sheepish look crosses his face. It probably looks like he had been out here fighting and having fun instead of trying to come in and help. At least, that's what his inner critic says to him. Truth is, Grey had just figured out a way to dissipate the fight when the door from the flophouse opened into the alley and half his team spilled out.

Grey is happy they are ok. He sizes them up; June seems to have taken a blow or two herself, and Charles has a package on his shoulder.

"Who's that?" Grey says, pointing at the man on Charles.

"It's the guy we are looking for actually. How's that for a score? The one who snatched the Mata Hari woman, and brought her here." Rosa says.

Grey rubs his chin and turns to look at the sailors, they all grin sheepishly.

"What happened here?" Rosa asks.

"A misunderstanding." Grey replies. He finally gets off the ground. As do three out of the four sailors; the other is hefted up, and his weight dispersed between two of the sailors; they head off down the alley. The last sailor, the indecisive one, gives Grey a look like he knows something. . .then pops Grey a salute and hurries to catch up to his buddies.

"What was that look about?" Rosa says.

"Don't know Rosa, maybe he knows something is amiss or his instincts tell him something is up with us." Grey says.

"What do you mean something is up with us?" June asks, coming into the alley finally.

Charles grins at her, "Like we are different. Momma always told me, 'Don't be afraid to be different hon. People will look at you strangely, but that is just because they are jealous.'"

Not knowing what to say to that, June says nothing.

"So what was that about?" Rosa asks Grey again, her curiosity still aroused.

"They came out of a door into the alley, I was running full bore and we collided. A fight instantly ensued. There were too many for me to get away and they probably would've followed me anyway. They are pretty drunk. I kept pace until I had an idea." Grey says.

"What idea?" she asks.

Grey says, "Strange enough, I all could think of was the song 'What do you do with a drunken sailor, what do you do with a drunken sailor.' It was running over and over in my head while we were going at it. And then it clicked, befriend them! So I managed to stop the fight and did."

"Amazing." Charles says, "Never would'a thought of that."

"I just went whoa, whoa whoa.... And it stopped, then

we realized it, and that's when you guys came out. I'm glad it worked out that way." Grey says.

Great looks up and down the alley, "Let's get out of here, we can talk about it later. We have to hand off Lee Batard and get you and June to the ball. I won't pass up the opportunity to see you dressed up all formal and such." Grey says.

Charles looks sheepish and uncomfortable in his skin. With a lifetime spent in the shadows, he isn't used to dressing in a way as to grab attention. Rather the opposite actually. He knows he will be looked at and noticed, although he tells himself they will all be looking at June.

The team heads back through the alleys, towards the town's only hotel. They need to get back. The team isn't going to leave Mata Hari flapping in the wind just because they have their jewels. There is more to this mission than jewels and a bastard of a man.

CHAPTER TWENTY-THREE

Having yet to come up with any plan of action Miokel, John, Agnuni and his Armenian-French Foreign legion of four, all stand on the balcony outside of Lee Batard's room. Miokel and Agnuni are discussing the possibilities as to where Lee Batard may be.

John has managed to strike up a connection with a couple of the legionnaires and they are checking out the women on the street down below. Finding a similarity in their crassness, they keep pointing out to each other the ones they like.

Mackenzie and the other Legionnaire seem to be in duty mode and are watching the goings on below, constantly scanning up and down the street.

It is Mackenzie that spots them first, "There they are!" she says, leaning over the balcony and pointing at them in her excitement.

The rest of the team comes out of the alley across from the hotel, Charles has a human package on his shoulder and Grey is all dirty, the rest of the team seems just fine.

After just a second of looking, Miokel and Agnuni head back into the hotel room and out the hall, heading for the back stairs; they hurry to meet the team in the hotel's alley. Mackenzie, John and the other legionnaires follow in their wake.

Miokel and Agnuni spill out of the door as Grey and the rest of the team arrive; within seconds, the alley is alive with chatter, catch up conversation and chaotic energy. All are talking at the same time, each telling their stories of the last hour. After about five minutes of this, Grey motions to Charles to take June inside so they can get ready for the next part of the mission. Their departure seems to help subside the energy and chaos of the moment.

Lee Batard, who must've been awakened by the chaos suddenly chooses this moment to leap off of Charles' shoulder and attempt an escape. The team quickly traps him between them and the legionnaires. Seeing the futility of any attempted action, he turns his attention to Agnuni and attempts to plead his case.

"I am a representative of France!" he says to Agnuni, "I am Lee Batard, a representative of France! You must do as I say!" He points at Grey and his team, "Shoot these people, they are attempting to prevent my mission." Lee Batard gestures angrily at Grey, Rosa, and Charles, he singles each of them out with his hand. When he gets to Mackenzie and John, he stops. A question crosses his face...

"Who are you?" he asks John. John blinks at him, he has nothing to say to this man, although he is curious as to how he escaped Johns watchful eye. John doesn't ask because he knows it is because he was watching the woman below, more than he was paying attention to the goings-on inside Lee Batard's room.

Agnuni speaks to Lee Batard directly, "We know who you are; we received a wire from France directly. It said to take you into custody and ship you out to France. It also said you do not have the authority or permission to act as an agent of France. Nor are you who you say you are."

Agnuni turns to him legionaries, "Take him to the ship." He commands.

The local authorities grab him and start to drag him away; Lee Batard keeps screaming at them, "I am the bastard! I am the bastard! I am the ..." WHACK! One of the legionnaires had had enough. He silenced the bastard with one blow.

"If you really are the bastard, then you deserve it more than she." He says to him; the legionnaires start beating the bastard with their clubs.

Chef Agnuni turns to Miokel, and takes on a military posture, salutes Miokel. Miokel looks Agnuni in the eyes, expressing gratitude and connection, and nods his head.

Without further pomp and circumstance, Chef Agnuni pivots and leaves. Catching up to his men and figuring they have beaten their captive enough, he commands them to get Lee Batard to the steamer ship without further delay.

CHAPTER TWENTY-FOUR

Not wanting to miss a moment of this extravagant affair, June and Charles arrive at the ballroom exactly one minute before the event was scheduled to start. Accolades to the hotel, they were actually ready when they arrived. June and Charles were the first guests by a full fifteen minutes much to Charles' chagrin.

It is all part of June's master plan; she had convinced Charles to arrive at her room 15 minutes ago and was ready when he arrived. That told Charles everything he needed to know about her excitement, in spite of the earlier affairs. He is pretty sure it wasn't about her getting to meet with Mata Hari again either.

Although June is from a time frame about 40 years from now and she may know the significance of this action they are putting in motion, he is pretty sure she is excited about seeing all the glam and glitter of this high-tooted affair, and not any possible world changing effects of their mission.

Charles is actually glad about that and has decided to do his best to enjoy it as well. It's not something he would normally attend (by a long shot) and since he is attending with a beautiful young woman about half his age, he knows he will be the envy of all the pompous asses in attendance. He will enjoy that more than anything, and plans on playing it up at every opportunity.

He glances down at the flowers tied to her wrist. When Charles arrived at June's room, she was finishing up some kind of flower arrangement she made out of the remnants of the flowers. She trimmed some up, added some of the green leaves and arranged it all together with some ribbon. He tied it to her wrist for her and they were off to the ball as soon as she stopped hugging and thanking him!

Finally, after about 15 minutes of being the only ones at the ball, the floodgates open to the ballroom. Apparently everyone, in their efforts to be fashionably late, arrives at the same time. Their efforts to be noticed and special have proven to be an exercise in futility unless of course their efforts were to impress June. For she stood at attention, with good sight-lines at the entrance, watching everyone enter, and mentally critiquing their outfits and picturing said outfits on her body's figure. You never know when you might need outfit ideas after all.

Charles nudges her.

"Ouch! I know she's here. I can tell you the outfit and time of arrival for everyone in the ballroom." June glares at Charles causing him to look a little sheepish.

"Sorry madam, didn't mean to insult." A smirk escapes his face.

June wraps her arms around his and hugs her head into his shoulder as one would her father, "None taken, just nervous I guess. Plus, I am really sore from earlier." She puts her hand on her bosom absentmindedly, the bruising and swelling in process reminding her of her   dire situation a short while ago.

"Want to talk about your favorite outfit? Mine is yours..." Charles says, wanting to distract her from her pain and bring that smile back to her face. He knows she is loving this part of the mission.

She smiles at him.

"No, let us get this show on the road. I will just get nervous if I wait, so let's 'do this' as Rosa would say." June adds, "I am ready."

Without hesitation Charles puts his hand on hers and starts walking, standing tall and proper like those around him, he even manages to get his nose in the air a bit.

Meandering their way through the crowd, stopping for some small talk on the way so as to not be too obvious, Charles and June make their way over to Mata Hari, who is mingling with random people since her "date" has failed to show as of yet.

June and Charles make their way to her, "Good evening Mi Lady." June says to her. Charles nods his body in greeting. Not saying a word, while looking about the room.

"Do you have time to talk?" June asks of her.

Nervous, her eyes dart about, "I cannot. I cannot, not be here when he gets here." Mati Hari says.

"You have nothing to fear." June says to her.

Mata Hari's eyes get big and fearful, "You are mistaken my fellow concubine. Mine is not as fair as yours." she says, pointing at Charles.

June hesitates, not wanting to get into it here, instead preferring a private place, in case it turns into a scene.

"He, we ... are here for a reason." June says.

Mata Hari looks across the room at Agha Petros, who

happens to be the person being driven around town in the car earlier. "You might want to walk away. In fact, best that you do so. Things are not as they seem."

June takes a risk and Charles saying nothing, standing there with her arm in his, he is doing his job.

"He's not coming. He uh. . .he tried something earlier and well...." June says.

Charles helps her out, "He is a bastard and is getting his just deserves. He tried hurting Ms. Dearg and that was that. We..." June puts her hand on his arm to stop him.

"Please come with me, we will all be safe now." June says.

Mata Hari looks from June to Charles. She sees a brotherly, sisterly love before her and not a concubine, physical relationship. She says to June, "Come with me. There is a beautiful cafe nearby. We can sit and chat there for a bit."

Charles lets them walk off alone, and scoping the room, he makes his way over to the refreshments. He grabs some punch and a few hand snacks, before heading out of the ballroom to watch from afar.

*****

Leaving the ballroom together June and Mata Hari make their way to the cafe. Closed this time of day, it is a perfect spot for a private conversation. They nod to the bellmen on their way through. None of them feeling inclined to remind the two beautiful women that the cafe is closed, preferring instead to take in the wafting scents they left in their wake. It is as close as the bellmen will come to experiencing one of these women, and they will not ruin the moment.

Mata Hari says, "So I know you are not who you say you are..."

Grey had prepared June for this moment.

"None of us are." is June's reply.

Grinning in spite of herself, Mata Hari loves her answer, "True, true Ms. Dearg, which means red by the way, did you know that? It is a good name for a concubine, isn't it?"

June glares at her and then remembers her cover as one. Damn, gotta remember these things. Smiling, she responds, "It is indeed, this way I don't have to waste time with men who are not into redheads. You know what I mean? Nothing like taking a trip by boat, train and car, only to be turned away because of your hair, and the spirit that goes with it."

Suddenly Mata Hari is wondering if this Ms. Dearg is in exactly the same boat as she, Mata Hari decides to stop testing her and see what she wants. Waving her hand dramatically she says, "Well, enough of that."

She looks at June, "What exactly is it that I can do for you?"

"You have connections that we don't have time to develop. We would like you. . .I would like you to send a telegram or convince one of your old favorites to do it." June says.

"Which old favorite?" she asks.

"An old German favorite." June answers.

"I have only one old German favorite, Mr. Zimmerman. He is a little rough, yet really good to me. I was always taken care of by him."

"Yes, I don't want you to do him harm, just have him

send a message." June says.

"Yes, I see. Where is this telegram headed and what does it need to say?" She asks.

"That's a good question, and I will answer it, it's a long answer, though! I also know we can help you out and I am being literal!" June says

Mata Hari tilts her head in surprise, "Why would you help me?"

"Why wouldn't we help you?" June replies.

CHAPTER TWENTY-FIVE

Grey puts his arm around June. They walk right out the front door, those beautiful doors she remembers admiring on the way in. She loves fine architecture. Now though, what she would love more than anything, is a drink.

Using her hand to grab Grey's arm and remove herself from it, she instead hooks her hand on his inner elbow. Looking up at the giant of a man she asks, "Do we have time to stop for a drink? I could really use one."

He looks down at her and sees she is serious. "I believe we do, in fact, our rendezvous point is right across the street from one. Let's adjourn there my lady."

"Good" she replies, "I look forward to one good stiff drink with all of us. This is an interesting thing we do, this job. Interesting...."

Still walking in his arm, she relishes the safe feeling of it. Even in these streets, this time of the night and perhaps on any street at any time of night.

*****

The rest of the team arrives at the meet point in short

succession. Grey, across the street in the café with June, gets Miokel's attention by making eye contact through the window. Miokel walks them across the street to the gnarly looking indoor cafe.

The outside is adorned in ancient stucco with layer after layer of 30-year-old paint falling off, in all its repetitive shades and colors; the cafe, never the less, seemed the most welcoming place around. The team walks through the open arched entryway and turn right to where June and Grey have claimed the window seating area. The facade of the structure, currently on the shady side of the sun, allows for a cooler breeze to form and it meanders through the open window into the cafe and out the rear door of the structure. It's almost as if the sun on that side is demanding the cooler air to come its way; Enticing it to its will.

As the team gathers around the small table, the area is engulfed briefly by the terrifying screeching sound that only moving chairs can make.

June motions to the café owner and the old man brings over the drinks. Gliding effortlessly, he manages to weave through the team and place the tray on the table and not a drop spilled. Without making eye contact, he pulls a spin move and departs quickly.

Grey addresses the team, "I think June scared him when she tried talking to him. She forgot she doesn't speak the local language."

"He looked at me like I was speaking alien or something. Although I think part of it was a woman speaking period."

Grey says, "That was definitely part of it, not to mention being a bodacious, redheaded, white woman either!"

The team laughs.

"So what's up, why are we here instead of heading to our jump point"? Rosa asks.

"This is Junes' thing actually." Grey answers.

After just a slight pause, June says, "I just wanted to take a moment and say to all of you how much I love working with you and am grateful to have found you and..." getting teary eyed, she loses the words. Instead, everybody reaches for their shot glass and raises them, "Here, here and other sappy stuff." says John.

"Here, here."

"Damn we are corny." Charles says to Rosa.

"Yes, we are." She replies, elbowing him, "Go with it."

After the moment passes, June asks Grey, "All this was to get her to send a telegram?"

"Yes, well and the contents of those bags I am sure." Grey says.

"All this for a telegram." She says again, not getting it.

Miokel chimes in, "If I may?" he asks Grey, receiving a nod and grin, "I was hoping you would chime in."

"Andrew Zimmerman is responsible for a telegram sent to the Mexican government, trying to entice them into attacking the United States. Basically saying they, the Germans, are getting ready to attack any and all U.S. Ships on the oceans. They will be so busy and occupied reproducing the goods sunk on those ships, and defending the remaining ships, that this will be a good time for Mexico to attack the United States from the south. Most say this telegram, and one or two other events, were the deciding factors in the United Sates actively entering WW1." Miokel says.

"How would this be to their advantage?" she asks, "Why would they want another superpower getting involved in a war against them?"

"Who says this is in their best interest?" Miokel says.

"It's in somebody's best interest or we wouldn't be here." June says.

Mackenzie, in her own world, says, "You, have entered, the Twilight zone."

"What?" John looks at her.

Blushing, "Sorry..." Mackenzie says.

"No. No sorry. What did you say?" John asks.

Mackenzie says, "I said, you have entered the Twilight Zone. Or in other words, you have entered an area that is not easily explained."

"Where things are not black and white; it is not just right and wrong, yet somewhere in between." Miokel says.

"Well no, not exactly," Mackenzie replies, "More like, an even bigger picture. I know I am the youngest of the group, yet I think that gives me an advantage in this line of thinking. All that schooling is still in my head." She says, "Economics and all that."

Miokel's eyes go wide, getting it.

Mackenzie smiles, "Yes, exactly. Economics. Imagine if all of Europe and Asia were beating each other into oblivion and the United States managed to stay out of it. The US would make tons of money producing goods and utilizing their resources for profit. Maybe the United States would've been the only superpower left after the German war machine ate up all the rest of the Worlds' resources and humans." She says.

"But who would have the forethought about all that, and have the resources to..." June says.

"The PAB's." the team says in unison.

"Ok, ok. Enough of that." Grey says laughing, "You guys are going to get yourselves in trouble with all of this out-of-the-box and big picture thinking. Let's just focus on getting back to what's becoming our second home. We are not out of the woods yet."

Silence for a bit.

June ponders many things and just has to ask one more question, "This is huge it seems. There must be some kind of guarantee that this Zimmer man?!" she asks, unsure of his name, "Sends this telegram. Perhaps we are going there next to make sure he does?" she asks of Grey.

"That is beyond my need to know my dear. Or perhaps there is another team there now." Grey replies.

"You mean we aren't the only team?" Mackenzie exclaims, "How many are there?"

"That is not on my need to know list either Mac." He says, "Let's just go with, more than one."

CHAPTER TWENTY-SIX

The team enters the alley behind their original arrival point. Walking the alley full of junk and smelling of human and animal, they pick and choose their path carefully. It has been a crazy busy couple of days; the entire team is tired and ready for their five days off. First they must negotiate the poop land-mines randomly dispersed through-out the alley.

Succeeding, they enter the walled in area behind their building. The Kangal dog next door apparently excited about their arrival pokes his head over the wall. Seeing him, Charles smiles and takes a moment to say hello. Giving him a good scratch just behind the ears, he thanks him for saying hello and for the heck of it adds, "Thanks for watching our backs, we appreciate it."

The rest of the team too tired to stop and play, enter the back door of the building. Grey stops and holding the door, looks at his invisible watch. "Come on Charles, we gotta go. We are pushing it this time!"

A car enters the far end of the alley. There are men hanging off all parts of it. Between them, the driver and his passenger, there are eight men on the convertible. It races its way down the alley.

"Ok, coming!" Charles says. He jogs to catch up and runs through the doorway. Grey walks through and lets the door close naturally behind him.

The car skids to a halt, Agha Petros and his men have arrived, behind the team just a bit; he and his men pull up in the alley as the back door closes. They pile off the vehicle and enter the walled yard.

The Kangal dog next door was waiting. He jumps over the wall and runs towards the back door, his aim to get between them and the door to the inside. His massive frame a block between them and what is inside.

Agha Petros winds his way through his men to get to the front of the pack. The dog snarles at him; purpose in his face, he is not going to allow them to enter, that is obvious!

Behind the dog, noise and dust escape the cracks of the doors.

Agha Petros pulls his pistol and levels it at the dog. One of his men puts his hand out, in motion. "One moment, one moment. He is ours, Sir. The dog that is." He proceeds to remind him, they use him next door to protect the livestock when they get their hands on some.

Perplexed, Agha pauses.

The wind sounds coming from behind the door crescendo to a dull roar, and the white dust forces its way out of the cracks between the door and frame.

"Why does this dog protect them?" Agha Petros asks.

"Perhaps it is not as it seems sir?" the man answers.

A myriad of lights seek the outdoors through the cracks in the door, greens, reds, purples, and yellow shades flash briefly, each taking a turn making their presence known.

Agha Petros stands and watches. He has no idea what to think of what he sees. He knows this building, it is his, like most of the buildings in this town. This room has been empty for a long time. He does not know why, but he is called to leave it that way. Every time someone suggests a use for it, he says, "No. It must remain as it is." That is his answer and he doesn't know why just that it is.

"Perhaps." Agha Petros says.

He holsters his pistol. That strange man that had befriended him during his rounds had told him about seven people that were here to steal his town from him. They had plans to take it over he said. He had been very convincing, but in hindsight, what does that mean? His instincts had told him it was not true, but he had to check it out anyway.

The noise inside has subsided. The dog without warning relaxes, looks at Agha Petros, and then walks off and out the back gate, his work here is done, he and his world's strongest bite head off for a nap in some shade. His men enter the building, but Agha Petros already knows what that outcome will be. They are gone, out the front of the building. It is obvious or the dog would not have let them in. Having better things to do, he walks off and heads back to his car. He will wait for the already known news there.

CHAPTER TWENTY-SEVEN

Agnuni, the Armenian legionnaire, approaches the steamer, one of his men walks behind him with their package in his secure control. The captive is in a sorry state and having issues walking. The legionnaire is dragging the prisoner, more than anything.

Reaching the bottom of the gangplank, Agnuni seeks permission to come aboard, "Hello, the ship!" he calls out.

After a moment, a couple of sailors appear, all of them seem to have been fighting recently; showing bruises on the face and scrapes on the knuckles.

One of them seems to be in charge.

"Well, what do we have here?" the Captain asks while pointing at their captive.

"She cannot answer you, Captain. Her jaw is broken and wired shut." Agnuni says.

The Captain reacts in shock. The legionnaire mistakes it for horror, "It was not I, Captain sire, even I am way above that. I would not do that, many other things, but not that."

"Aye, I see that sir. No worries, I meant not to accuse, just shock and surprise, you may not treat woman as such.

Unless she whole-heartedly deserves it, such as this one must've." The Captain says.

"Yes, yes, surely did." Agnuni replies.

"Where is her representative of France?" the Captain asks.

"Alas, he did not make it sire." Agnuni answers.

"What a shame." The Captain answers.

"If you say so sir." Agnuni having no love lost for the likes of Lee Batard.

The steamer Captain smiles. "Bring her aboard. We have been waiting for her return." he says, "Will you be joining us for the journey?"

"We will sir. Since her escort is no longer with us, we will ensure she is re-deposited in the rightful place, and explain it all to the powers back in France." he says. Agnuni is anxious to get this over with and cuts the pleasantries short.

"Permission to come aboard Captain?" Agnuni says.

"Permission granted." He answers, waving them to come about simultaneously.

The legionnaires walk the gangplank onto the steamer. Their package is deposited unceremoniously onto the deck. Unable to stand, it lay there in a heap.

"What a pity." The Captain says.

"Again, it wasn't us Captain." The legionnaire says.

The Captain leans down to look into the captive's eyes, mostly swollen, they do manage to look out at him and even through the tiny slits, he can see them pleading at him. "Obviously, there are some in the world who would. Who am I to judge the details of the spy world, I am but a lowly steamboat captain." he says.

The Captain kneels down so that he is ear level with the

captive; he leans in closer so that he is next to the far ear. The ear away from the legionnaire, so he cannot hear what he is about to say, "No soup for you, Lee Batard, no soup for you."

Standing back up, the Captain says to all, "There was a red sky this morn, tis a stormy day to come for sure. We will batten down the hatches." and turning to the legionnaires he says, "Perhaps if you would chain her to the deck, this way if it gets to rough she will not wash overboard and rob France of her penance?"

"Then we can all go below and play some cards perhaps?" The legionnaire requests.

"We can dear sir, we also have a fair supply of wine and it may even be appropriate to consider my stash of absinthe. Storms are great times for games of Hijinks my dear sirs." the Captain says.

Agnuni motions for the Armenian legionnaire to chain her to the deck, while he and the Captain adjourn to the bridge.

The prisoner suddenly comes to life, using their last ounces of strength, the prisoner kicks and screams. The legionnaire asks the other crew members for help. Obliging, they drag the prisoner kicking and managing to scream somehow through the wired jaw. They drag him over to the bow of the boat, thrusting him roughly against the metal rail, Lee Batard is knocked unconscious.

The crew member says, "Let's get her chained and go inside for the hijinks."

"Agreed!" says the legionnaire.

The crew member throws a tarp onto the unconscious hump of broken human being laying there on the deck and catches up to the others already headed inside.

CHAPTER TWENTY-EIGHT

The woman is dressed in light, flowing desert attire, native to the nomads of the area. She stands on the dune, the setting sun afore her. It burns its vivaciousness into her face. She stands with eyes closed, reveling in its ferocity. Letting it warm her retinas and imprint its light onto them.

She has no idea who those people were. Perhaps they were sent angels. Who knows? It feels that way to her. How else would they know where she was, and who she is? Why else would someone save her, a used up, thrown away concubine? And all they needed her to do was send a telegram to Arthur. She had forgotten about him.

He was pretty good to her, a little kinky, but good to her just the same. A strange German man, strong and secure as many are. Arthur Zimmermann was his full name. He had come into her life. . .well, let's leave it at that. What she remembers most is how he would straighten and pull at his mustache while he thought. He was a thinker and had plans to help his mother Germany take over the world.

Why those people were so sure he would do as she

asked is beyond her. "He will" is all Ms. Dearg and that giant gray-bearded man kept saying. Great confidence in the least! No matter how it turns out, it is no matter to her. They were not concerned with results before setting her free as Lee Batard was. She is doubtful he would've followed through with her release, instead using her until she was no longer pertinent. Lee Batard then surely would have disposed of her.

As soon as Mata Hari sent the telegram, the mysterious ones set her free. In fact, when the three of them came out of the telegraph office, there stood a Persian man, holding the halter of a lead horse. The clothes she is now wearing were bundled to the plain saddle. This man said nothing, he simply smacked the horse on the ass when she and Ms. Dearg intended on turning the goodbye into a long affair. She swears she heard him speaking English to the tall gray-bearded man as she raced off, something about schedules....

One hand at her side and the other stretched behind her holding the reins of a well-trained, hard run horse. She will have to clean him up nice tonight, he deserves it. Tied to this horse is another, ladened with supplies: food and water, enough for one human and her horses for a week.

The wind picks up as the sun goes down. Small unseen specks of sand bite at her face, the wind swirls the yellow sands at her feet, picks it up and spins it around her exposed toes and ankles, her bare legs and feet have no protection. She feels it hop and skip in tornado fashion up her legs to her knees before the flowing robe cuts off the wind's power. Her legs feel the raw skin inducing sandpaper effect of the sharp minuscule crystals. She will have to figure out how to wrap the provided cloth leggings into protective footwear tonight, her legs won't take a full day of sun exposure and abrasive sand. In the meantime, it reminds her she is no longer forgotten and dying in her own waste, she is as free as she can make herself out to be. All she has to do is survive the desert and her life is back in her hands.

Life is good; she is free from all human binds. Not ready to pick a direction, she moves down the dune, out of the winds and into the oasis to secure a place for the night.

She will figure out tomorrow, tomorrow.

CHAPTER TWENTY-NINE

The storm rages, the steamboat rises and falls with every tremendous wave, tiny round specks of light float up and down with each wave.

Inside this boat of tightly bonded strips of wood, the crew does their best to keep track of their game of hijinks, and alcohol laded drinks. The sea does its damnedest to keep them busy.

Joyful and victories they laugh and banter, having fun in the craziness of the storm.

Up on the deck the storm rages, the wind howls, and the salt water spray works its way into every nook and cranny of the ship and anything on deck. Anything not lashed down securely, moves and creaks as the boat ungulates and flexes with the waves.

At the bow of the boat, a tarp flaps and rages, waving angrily at the storm; loose and lashed in only a couple spots, it beats the contents below it relentlessly.

The contents under it shrink against the foremost bow of the steamboat, trying to wedge itself against the points for support. Shivering relentlessly, he prays to his devils for warmth. They will protect him and keep him alive until he is needed again. He has faith in that. The devils need him.

the end. . .till next time

ABOUT THE AUTHOR

C.M. Halstead is the product of 40 plus years of travel and exploration; a childhood as an Air Force brat and service in the Marine Corps changed him forever. He managed 84 people, negotiated multi-million dollar contracts, drove Jeeps professionally — usually at crazy angles and locals.

An astute believer in adventure, he is now doing the craziest thing ever, pursuing his passion full out and becoming an accomplished author.

Ready or not, here he comes!

Are you ready to join in as he takes you on one wild ride after another? Free your mind to worlds that may or may not be reality and let your imagination be ignited by C.M. Halstead.

For other works by the author check out cmhalstead.com or any other of your favorite book sources.

Other works to include:

TRIP WALK: Book one of The Tripper Series, this book sets the tone for the series, the book's introduction sets the tone for the author on the series and his perspective on life.

EARNED INNOCENCE: A military fiction book about the loss of innocence, coming of age, and the effort it takes to face the demons of war in order to return all the way home.

The musings of the author can also be found at cmhalstead.com or various social media sources:

Twitter: @CM_Halstead
Facebook: CMHalsteadAuthor
Instagram: CM_HALSTEAD

9 780986 344558